MARIA

by

Arleta Richardson

Light and Life communications

MARIA
BY ARLETA RICHARDSON
COVER ILLUSTRATION ©1998 BY SUSAN SCHULTZ

ISBN 0-89367-227-0

Light and Life Communications
Indianapolis, IN 46253-5002
Printed in the U.S.A.

Dedicated in the memory of
Maria Mannoia
to the
pastors, early pilgrims and children
of the mission, many of whom are
still serving the church.

Arleta Richardson

General Conference - 1999
Anderson, Indiana

Dedicated to the memory of

[illegible]

to the [illegible]

[illegible] early pilgrims and characters

of the missionary [illegible]

[illegible] church.

TABLE OF CONTENTS

INTRODUCTION

Between 1890 and 1900, 3.6 million immigrants arrived in the United States. Of that number, 1.6 million settled in the Chicago area. The first and second decades of the 20th century would see an even greater influx of families, especially from Europe. This was true in spite of an immigration law passed in 1917 over President Wilson's veto that required all newcomers to pass a literacy test.

With these new citizens came their languages, cultures, lifestyles and religions. The differences they brought with them as they settled in the large cities and the smaller villages surrounding them caused the formation of ghettos. "Little Italy" in the Chicago area was the ghetto into which the Mannoia family moved. The comfort of finding *compadres* who shared their likes and dislikes, language, ways of doing things and religious beliefs was not to be underestimated.

Imagine then, the anger, unrest and strong adverse reaction directed toward any who dared to reject one of these values.

Reverend Forest C. Bush, Sr., a former pastor of the mission and later Illinois Conference Superintendent, notes:

"In those early days there was a great deal of intensity in the feelings expressed toward any of the community that dared to convert to a Protestant church. Sister Mannoia had the strength of personality and the mental ability to stand her ground and provide a source of stability for many others who were not equally endowed."

Indeed she did. During the years before World War II, there was no reason to doubt that the Roman Catholic Church carried on a program of persecution just as Maria recorded in her journal. In small villages such as Melrose Park and "Little Italy," the word of the church and the priests was the law of the people. Their belief in the rightness of the church and its leaders was sincere and deeply ingrained. Few would be bold enough to challenge the rulers or the priests, and fewer still would actually withdraw from the faith. The result of doing so was relentless persecution, and not many were willing or able to endure it.

These are the years through which Maria Mannoia and her family persevered and triumphed. Since that time, a gradual ecumenical spirit has grown between Catholics and Protestants, and such circumstances are rare in American churches today. Although church theology and polity differ, the belief of both in the sovereignty of God and salvation through Christ Jesus makes it possible for them to work together amicably in their communities and ministerial associations.

It is true, as Proverbs 31 states of a godly woman, that "her children arise up and call her blessed, and her husband also, and he praiseth her" (v. 28-29, KJV paraphrase). There is no greater blessing a mother could receive than to see each of her children serving God and working in His ministry. Maria was so blessed.

I am grateful to each of them for written remembrances and encouragement as I worked on the book:

Rose Mannoia Scittine, Dominic Mannoia (deceased, 1994), Joe Mannoia, Anne Mannoia Esposito (deceased, 1997), V. James Mannoia, Mary Mannoia Chapman.

In addition I received help from:

Reverend Forest C. Bush, Sr.; Ken and Florence Stevens; Alice Bandringa Terman; Robert A. Traina; Reverend K.M. Walton.

I have been blessed by becoming acquainted with this dedicated woman over the past year as I have lived with her through her journal and the words of her family and friends. The remarkable talent she possessed in being able to produce a couture garment by careful examination of the original was, I believe, reflected in her own life. The spirit of Christ was reproduced in Maria as she studied the Original.

Through the Maria Mannoia Scholarship Fund at Asbury Theological Seminary in Wilmore, KY, a number of young men and women have the opportunity to prepare themselves to serve their day as Maria served hers — selflessly and tirelessly presenting the claims of Christ to a broken and hurting world.

The family's prayer and mine is that Maria's life may so touch the readers that they may say with her, "I thank the Lord that He has separated me with joy. I am content … and now the Lord has prepared for me the crown for that day. Amen. Amen."

"Remember those earlier days after you had received the light, when you stood your ground in a great contest in the face of suffering. Sometimes you were publicly exposed to insult and persecution; at other times you stood side by side with those who were so treated. So do not throw away your confidence; it will be richly rewarded. You need to persevere so that when you have done the will of God, you will receive what he has promised. For in just a very little while,

'He who is coming will come and will not delay.
But my righteous one will live by faith.
And if he shrinks back, I will not be pleased with him.'

But we are not of those who shrink back and are destroyed, but of those who believe and are saved."

Hebrews 10:32, 33, 35-39

PROLOGUE

A MISSIONARY RETURNED FROM HIS FIELD AND settled in an area west of Chicago following World War II. Still possessed of an evangelist's heart, he searched for a small town where he might witness for the Lord. He finally decided upon Melrose Park. As he went from door to door to present the claims of Christ to this predominantly Italian community, he was met repeatedly by the same welcome.

"Oh! Do you know Maria? She has already been here."

As he trudged from house to house, the missionary was forced to ask himself, *Who is this woman?*

"This woman" was Maria Mannoia. As a young, devout woman she had immigrated from Sicily with her two small children and settled in "Little Italy." Maria was a leader, an activist, a feminist and a crusader before these traits were common among women. Following her conversion to Protestantism, her ceaseless efforts resulted in countless souls being touched by the Holy Spirit and brought to a knowledge of God.

Throughout the years Maria worked to bring God to her community through the Italian mission and church as well as through individual contacts. She suffered unbelievable persecution from the Roman Catholic Church, various government officials, angry neighbors and those who would have run her out of town if possible. Maria stood firm in confrontation with everyone from her husband to the Mafia.

As a result, she continues to influence the world through her children, grandchildren and the generations following. Truly the world she touched sees what God can do with a woman fully committed to Him and the advancement of His kingdom.

CHAPTER ONE

MARIA REMEMBERS

MARIA STOOD AT THE GATE IN FRONT OF THE brick bungalow on 21st Avenue, Melrose Park and watched the car disappear around the corner of Main Street. She hadn't intended to cry when Jimmy and his family left. After all, hadn't she given him to the Lord 40 years ago with the understanding that this precious son would go where God called him? She wiped her eyes with the handkerchief she had been waving and turned toward the house God had provided for her.

The Lord knows I am only human, she thought as she climbed the 13 steps to the porch. She smiled when she remembered that her daugher Anne had always declared that there were at least a hundred steps when she had to clean them each week.

Brazil was so far away, so unknown. But she trusted God to care for her family. He had never failed her — never. Quite suddenly her mind returned her to a time and place she had known as a young girl of 16. She remembered so vividly.

MISILMERI, IN THE PROVINCE OF POLERMO, clung to the side of a hill overlooking the Mediterranean Sea. The island of Sicily sparkled in the sun, and as Maria hung over the balcony surrounding the solarium of the great stone house in which she lived, the young girl thought that there could not be a more beautiful place on God's earth. The church bells pealed across the village, and from where she stood, Maria could see people hurrying toward the Catholic church on the *stradone* (main street).

She had attended mass at daybreak, as was her custom, and now the rest of the bright day stretched before her. She called to her friend Francesca on the street below.

"Good morning, Franci. What will you do today? Is there time to go to the *Castello* (castle)?

Franci waved to her. "Later perhaps, to watch the sun go down. I have errands for Mama this morning. What will you do?"

As if in answer to Franci's question, the voice of Maria's older sister, Josephine, came clearly from below.

"Maria! Paoló is coming with the goats. Is the container ready?" Maria wrinkled her nose at the interruption and clattered down the narrow staircase to the kitchen.

"Anita could have gotten the milk, Josephine. Why do I have to run to the door from the second floor?"

She snatched the pail from the pantry and grabbed a couple of *lira* from the dresser where the dishes stood. By the time Paoló reached the house, Maria was sitting on the doorstep waiting for him.

"Too beautiful a day to work, Paoló. What do you say we take some bread and cheese to the hills and enjoy the sun?" she asked.

Paoló laughed as he milked the goat. "Easy for you, maybe, to spend the day in the hills. Can you imagine what would happen to me if Papa came home and found the goats not taken care of?"

He slung the small stool over his shoulder and retrieved the end of the rope tying the animals together. Maria watched as they picked their way along the rough, uneven cobblestones of the street. Lifting the milk pail, she returned to the kitchen. Mama was there with Josephine, and she smiled at Maria.

"Have you work for today?"

"Si, Mama. Signora Natta has brought a dress to alter. I would be working hard at this moment if Josie hadn't called me to do her chores."

She grinned at her sister, then ducked as Josephine flipped the towel in her direction. Maria scurried back up the stairs to the solarium, and soon the sound of her singing was heard in the village streets.

MARIA FELT FORTUNATE TO BE WELL EDUCATED as a professional seamstress. When her years in the local schools were completed, Papa had taken her to Palermo by burro and cart each week for two years to attend private school. In the beginning, Mama had been skeptical.

"Twenty *lira* a *week?* That's a lot of money for one so young. Shouldn't she wait a few years?"

"Wait for what, Mama? It isn't as though you really need me here. You have Vincenza to help with the work. Josephine is a good shopper, and both of them are wonderful cooks. The sooner I learn, the sooner I bring money to help the family."

Maria had prevailed, and her beautiful sewing was admired throughout the village.

"This is a welcome addition to our income," Papa told her. "You are a good daughter."

All her life was not devoted to her work, however. Maria was a devout member of the Catholic Church. Singing in the choir was a great joy for her. She spent many hours learning masses and, she was assured, "gained merits" for them.

Her defense of the church was fierce. No one questioned who would be the leader in a protest against the Salvation Army on a Saturday night. Maria was first to throw rocks and tomatoes at the group gathered on the street corner.

"Maria!"

The voice of her friend brought her to the balcony railing again.

Francesca stood on the street with her bundles. "There will be a dance tonight at the hall. Will you come, Maria?"

"Of course! Have I ever missed a dance?"

Francesca laughed. "Not that I remember. It wouldn't be the same without you. You aren't called the 'Ballerina of Misilmeri' for no reason! I will return in time for a walk to the hills this afternoon."

MARIA SAT DOWN IN HER QUIET KITCHEN AND looked at the familiar furniture around her. It seemed as though she could see her children surrounding the table and hear their bantering conversation. She would not trade those scenes for her early years in Sicily, but, ah! — those hills remained bright in her memory.

THE *CASTELLO* AT THE TOP OF THE HILL HAD long ago been a true castle. Later it became a jail, but now as the girls walked toward the abandoned shell of stone walls in the late afternoon sun, the area was used for picnics. Warm breezes caressed their cheeks and blew their hair as they sat looking out at the distant hills.

"The wind is in the right direction," Maria said. "Can you smell the sea?"

"I believe you could smell the sea if you lived in America," Francesca told her. "What I can smell are the grapes ripening."

Behind them on the hill were the vineyards of the Mannoia brothers, Niccolo and Vincenzo, where the two young men spent long days of hard work. Early in the morning, carrying a lunch of bread, cheese and a flask of wine, they trudged up the hill. It was often near dark before they returned in the evening.

Maria's eyes wandered over the lush vines.

"I hope Vincenzo and his brother will be free in time for the dance tonight."

"I'm sure they will. They seldom miss a party or a card game." Francesca laughed. "I don't think you care whether Niccolo shows up for the dance. We all know who has his eye on you. Has his family approached your father about a betrothal?"

Maria shook her head. "Papa would just tell them that I'm too young. Besides, the Mannoias need both boys to keep the vineyard going." Her face became serious.

"Francesca, does it worry you that the Mafia has become so powerful in Misilmeri? They demand money from the landowners, and no one dares defy them."

"I know. Papa says they promise protection, but who will protect us from them? We must keep our vineyards in order to live."

"I hear terrible stories about what could happen to those who refuse to pay." Sparks flew from Maria's dark eyes. "Someone needs to stand up to the 'capo' and tell him that we will no longer tolerate such treatment."

Francesca laughed at her friend. "You, Maria. You are the one to do that!"

SOONER THAN EITHER OF THE GIRLS COULD HAVE imagined, terrible things happened in Misilmeri. Papa returned home one evening, pale and shaken. He slumped into a chair by the kitchen table. Mama and the girls gathered around, expecting the worst.

"The Mannoias," Papa said. "A Mafioso approached Niccolo this week and ordered him to cut his neighbor's vines, because the man refused to pay them as required."

"'But that is his only livelihood,' Niccolo said, 'I can't do that.'"

"'There is no such thing as can't,' the Mafioso told him. 'You will do it or suffer the consequences.'"

"Niccolo would not bring ruin to his neighbor," Papa said. "And tonight as he stood in his doorway, the Mafioso walked by and shot him. 'An example to others,' he said."

The family was horrified. "Oh, Papa! Can't the priest do anything to help us?"

Papa shook his head. "Nothing."

"But what about Vincenzo? Will they come after him also?"

"Vincenzo is young and single. He will leave and go to America."

"America! So far away. Will we ever see him again?"

Maria remembered the years that followed. Fear remained in the village, and she was torn between relief that Vincenzo was safe in America and apprehension that he might not ever return to Sicily.

Vincenzo Mannoia *had* returned to the little village, and he had chosen the beautiful, strong-willed, happy-go-lucky Maria to be his wife.

After a courtship of six months, Maria and Vincenzo were married in the Catholic church and settled down to raise their family on the island that had nurtured them. All the memories of those years were not happy ones, Maria reflected. Of the five children born to them in Sicily, only Rosalina and Dominic had lived to come to America with her.

The year was 1913, she recalled. Life would never be the same for her after that. Some time before, Vincenzo had gone back to America to find a place for them.

"I do not feel at home here," he had told her. "Since Niccolo was killed by the Mafioso my heart is filled with anger toward them. I don't want to be on the same island with these men. We will make a new life for ourselves where we'll not be bothered again."

Mama and Papa had been grief-stricken. "Oh, Maria! So far away! We'll never see the children again. And what of your property? The houses and the vineyards?"

Maria shrugged. "He will leave them. It is not something we can carry with us. It is far away, but it is the thing Vincenzo needs to do. I am his wife, and I must go if he wishes."

On September 5, 1913, Maria, with Rosalina and Dominic, left Italy to sail to America. For 18 long days, the ship was their home. Dominic celebrated his first birthday on the voyage.

"Mama, will we still celebrate Dominic's birthday even if we aren't at home?"

"Of course, Rosie."

"He'll be so old when we arrive that Papa won't know him."

"He's having *one* birthday, not 10!" Mama told her. "Papa will know him all right. Dominic looks just like his father."

Maria recalled that it had not been an easy trip. There were many Italian families traveling to America to seek a fortune, a better life, or a new beginning. Rosie enjoyed the freedom of running about the ship, but to Maria the voyage was long and tiring. She was 31 years old when they arrived in Massachusetts.

Rosie looked about eagerly for her father.

"Isn't Papa going to meet us?"

"Not here, Rosie. We must take the train to the city of Chicago."

"Tonight, then."

Maria shook her head. "America is much bigger than our island of Sicily," she told her. "We can't travel across this country in one day."

The different languages were confusing to them. Although they listened for an Italian word or voice, nothing sounded familiar. Nine-year-old Rosalina spoke for all of them.

"I hope Papa has found a house in a village where

people speak Italian. We'll be talking to ourselves until we learn this new language."

Maria silently agreed, but the three day train trip across the country with their belongings was all she had time to think about.

Chicago was not a village. The noise of the huge train station with puffing steam engines and shouting people was overwhelming. They were both frightened and fascinated by the bustle of activity and unfamiliar crowds. Rosie held tightly to Maria's skirt as they made their way to the big waiting room above ground.

What a welcome sight it was to see Vincenzo anxiously scanning the stream of people who hurried past him. Rosie broke away from Maria with a happy shout.

"Papa! There he is! There he is!"

Life in America began for the Mannoia family.

CHAPTER TWO

THIS STRANGE NEW LAND

Father Benedict was exceedingly pleased as he paced slowly through the cloistered garden and courtyard of San Anselmo Church. This morning he was unaware of the heavy cross that swung from his belt, which was unusual, since he habitually repeated his morning prayers to the rhythm of the cross.

Today, however, other things occupied his mind. Although San Anselmo stood in the heart of an Italian Catholic community, the church had not been growing as one would expect with the arrival of more families from Italy than ever before. In spite of Father Benedict's best efforts, church attendance remained distressingly low. Needless to say, the income generated from the faithful few had not shown an inclination to rise.

These matters weighed heavily on the priest's heart. If (God forbid!) his parish should make a poorer showing than those in neighboring communities, it would reflect badly on his leadership.

The reason for his pleasure this morning could be directly traced to the arrival several months earlier of a new family to Dekoven Street. There was nothing about the young couple with two children to stir his interest; families such as theirs moved in regularly. He had been alerted to their presence by his associate Father John.

"A young man and his family by the name of Mannoia have moved into the house on Dekoven Street, Father."

"Mannoia?" The priest thought a moment. "I don't recall that name in our parish. Not related to anyone here, apparently. Where have they come from?"

"Sicily, I hear. The husband has been in America for some time. His family has just joined him."

"Good, good."

Within weeks, Father Benedict became aware that this name was being mentioned more often.

"Father, have you met Maria Mannoia?"

"You must hear Maria Mannoia sing, Father. She has the voice of an angel."

"Maria has opened her home to the ladies. What a wonderful seamstress she is!"

Gradually over the next few months, Father Benedict began to notice an increase in the number of ladies attending mass. Father John reported that the offerings were generous; whole families were participating in the services. Most gratifying!

"Could this be the influence of one woman that is causing a renewed interest in the church?" he asked Father John.

"It appears that way, Father. From what I hear, Maria is a leader in the community. Even though she goes out to work, she takes time daily to invite the neighborhood ladies to her home to pray. I've been told of a picture of Mary of Pompeii that she brought with her. They light candles and do the Novena religiously."

It was on these events that Father Benedict meditated this morning. Surely it was God's favor that brought the family to his parish at this time. A special prayer of thanksgiving was in order.

The object of these pleasant thoughts had not considered herself to be responsible for the growth in the local Catholic church. Actually, Maria had been miserable.

From the time they arrived at the Dekoven Street house in late September, 1913, the contrast between this place with wooden ceilings, stairs and door frames and her home in Sicily had served to increase her loneliness. She missed the cool stone walls and shuttered windows that had surrounded her since childhood. She grieved for her parents. She'd had no intention of ever leaving them and going to another country. Maria wept silently as she went about her business of settling the few belongings she was able to bring with her into these strange rooms. She expressed her unhappiness to Vincenzo.

"I hate it here in America! We had a good home and many friends in Sicily. We had family and our church. How could you believe that life here in this foreign place would be better? Where is the sea? Where are the mountains? There are no vineyards, and I've not seen a fig tree since we left home!"

Vincenzo was impatient. "What do you mean *we* had a family? *You* had a home and family! Have you forgotten what happened to mine? I notice that you failed to mention my only brother, murdered in cold blood by the Mafia. If I had not fled to America the first time, I would not be your husband today!"

"We had no trouble for eight years after you returned to Sicily," Maria retorted. "The vineyards were flourishing and we owned property. We have left it all — for what?"

In her heart Maria knew that danger from the Mafia still existed during those years, but she was unhappy. She was not ready to concede that the move had been necessary.

Vincenzo shrugged. "You have the children. You have your sewing. You have your church. What more do you want?"

"To return to my home," she muttered.

But Vincenzo didn't hear her. He had already left to join his compatriots at the pub across the street. *Just as well,* Maria thought. She wasn't feeling up to a full-scale battle with him.

As she became acquainted with the ladies in the neighborhood, Maria's natural good spirits began to return. She enjoyed the times that they prayed together before the small altar she had arranged. She found herself busy with sewing for many of them. Her neighbor Julia was especially impressed.

"Maria, your garments are better than we find in the store. Why don't you work for good wages?"

"I feel as though I have been sewing all my life." Maria replied. "I had wonderful training in Palermo. We learned pattern making, sewing and tailoring. I was able to support my family, even in a small town like Misilmeri. But I know nothing of a place to work here."

"Sidol Sewing Company. I'll show you where it is."

The Sidol Sewing Company was delighted to have a worker of Maria's ability. Her employer was quick to realize that here was a seamstress with unusual talent.

"Where did you learn to sew with so much skill? We seldom see such professional work in our factory."

Maria was pleased that her efforts were appreciated, but even going to the factory each day and caring for her family didn't take away the longing for home that she felt.

The year 1914 arrived with vague rumors of war and unrest in Europe. The news that Austrian Archduke Franz Ferdinand and his wife were assassinated in Sarajevo reached Chicago, but for the most part it was noted only in passing. What could an event so many miles away have to do with the new immigrants in America? There was no mention of Italy among the allies, and no danger that America itself could be involved. Other matters of interest to the young Mannoia family were about to occupy her thoughts.

One afternoon Maria returned from work and was preparing to fix dinner. Rosie, who had been watching and playing with Dominic, called her.

"Mama, there are some people at the door."

Maria wiped her hands and came from the kitchen.

"Saluto," (greetings) she said. "Please come in."

"I am Angelo Ricci. We have come to welcome you to the village." The pleasant young man was accompanied by his wife and three other *paisanos* (countrymen).

"Thank you," Maria answered him. "I've not seen you before. Do you attend the Catholic Church?"

Mr. Ricci shook his head. "No, we are Seventh Day Adventists. We'd like to talk to you about our faith. Are you familiar with the Bible?"

"In Italy I had a Bible," Maria told him. "I have memorized many things from it, and I know the Catechism."

"Then you know what it says about keeping the Sabbath Day holy."

Maria nodded. "Yes, I attend church every Sunday with my family."

"Ah, but Sunday is not the true Sabbath. The Bible tells us that the correct day to observe is Saturday. That is the seventh day on which God rested."

Maria stared at him blankly. She had not heard anything like that before. She listened carefully as these new people talked about religion.

"We would like to have you attend our services on Saturday," Mrs. Ricci told her. "We will come and take you with us."

"We will leave a Bible with you. If you will read it faithfully, you will learn what God has to say to you."

For some time Maria and the children attended the Seventh Day Adventist Church with her new friends. They continued to visit her home often. She liked to hear them when they spoke of God and His Word. Mostly they talked about the Sabbath. Maria wasn't knowledgeable about the things of the Bible, and she didn't find a lot of time to read it between going to work and taking care of her home.

One thing was plain to her. Vincenzo was not happy about this turn of events.

"You learn enough about religion from the priest," he said. "I don't trust these people. They will try to take you from your church. It's not good for you to be listening to them. You must not go to their services. They'll lead you away from the Catholic faith. Give back their Bible and don't see them again."

Maria was wise. There were times when she would stand up for her way, but this was not one of them. She didn't need trouble from her husband. Vincenzo was usually a quiet, mild-mannered man, but on occasion his wrath would descend upon the family, and it was not a pleasant sight. Reluctantly Maria broke off her friendship with the Adventist group and asked them not to visit her home again.

Gradually Maria's homesickness lessened, although she still missed her parents and longed to see them. Occasionally, too, her thoughts would return to the three babies that had died in Sicily before Dominic was born. They were to lose three more babies in America before the family was complete.

By 1917, news reached the Italian community that Italy was indeed involved in the World War. Neighbors who had come from the area of the country where battles were fought were concerned about loved ones at home. When it was learned that the Italians were defeated by Austro-German forces at Capporeto, a sadness hung over the community. For the family from Sicily, the war was still far away from their former home, and exciting things were taking place right in the house on Dekoven Street. In February, Joseph Mannoia arrived. Maria rejoiced that the baby was strong and healthy. As she rocked him, she recalled the day two years before when she thought she had lost her only son, Dominic. The scene was clear to her.

"Rose, watch your little brother while I hang out the clothes," she called up the stairs.

"Yes, Mama."

Maria's back was turned to the upper window, so she didn't see the little boy leaning out to look for his mama. Suddenly a scream from Rosie pierced the air, and Maria turned in time to see 3-year-old Dominic hit the ground and lie motionless. The next moments were a blur. The baby was dead — she was sure. Neighbors who heard the commotion came running, and all agreed that there was nothing to be done for the baby. He had fallen too far to possibly be alive.

Suddenly, however, Dominic began to breathe and was soon crying at the top of his voice.

"Well, he's not dead, Maria. Only live boys make that much noise."

Maria snatched him up and hugged him to her heart. "Thank God, thank God!" she cried. "He has been spared."

Dominic suffered no permanent damage, and now, at 5 years of age, he was ready for school.

Two years later, a daughter Anne was born. Maria kept busy with her growing family. There was no longer time to work at the sewing factory, but she continued to sew for others, as well as for her own family.

Rosie had become a young lady. At the age of 15, she felt privileged to have a mother who was a skilled seamstress. With her friends, Rose would study the latest fashions in the shop windows.

"Oh, wouldn't you love to have a dress like that, Rosie?"

"It would look perfect on you. But look at the price! Your papa would never buy that for you, would he?"

Rose looked at the dress carefully. "No, he couldn't afford that much for just one of us." *But I think I know a way to get it,* she thought to herself.

At home, Rose brought up the subject.

"Mama, there is the most beautiful dress in Patrini's window."

"Is that so?"

"It would be just the thing for the dance next week. Can you come and look at it?"

"I guess we could walk past there when we go out to shop."

Later, with the baby in the carriage and Joe hanging onto her skirt, Maria surveyed the creation in the window with a practiced eye.

"What color would you like?"

"A pretty blue, Mama. Wouldn't that be nice?"

A length of material was selected and carried home.

"Get the ball of string from the drawer, Rose. I'll take your measurements."

When supper had been cleared away, Maria spread newspaper on the table, and in a short time a pattern appeared, ready to be pinned to the new fabric. With deft fingers, Maria snipped and sewed. On the night of the dance, Rose appeared in an exact replica of the dress in the window.

"Oh, Rosie! Your papa did get that dress for you! How did you ever persuade him?"

Rosie shook her head. "No, this isn't the one in the shop. Mama made it for me."

"Your *mother* sewed it herself?"

"Yes, and made her own pattern, too. She can sew anything she looks at."

Rose had been named for her grandmother Mannoia. As the oldest child she often had responsibility for the younger children. Sometimes, though, one of them would be responsible for her.

"Mama, Peter has asked me to go out with him tonight."

"Do I know him?"

"He works at the pharmacy, Mama. He's a nice boy. May I go?"

Maria continued working on her sewing machine. "You may if Dominic goes with you."

"Dominic! I'm older than he is! Why should I drag him along on a date?"

"Two reasons," Maria responded calmly. "It looks better for a young girl to be accompanied by her brother rather than alone with a young man."

"What's the other reason?"

"Because I said so."

So Dominic went with the couple, as bored with the whole thing as Rose was annoyed. Her friendship with Peter grew, even under the supervision of her brother. When high school was over, Rose had another announcement for her parents.

"Pete and I want to get married."

"Married! When would this happen?"

"This summer, Mama."

"Rose, you are only 17 years old! I wasn't married until I was 22."

"That was the old country, Mama. This is America. I'm grown up. I've learned to take care of a house and children from you. Why should we wait another five years?"

After some discussion, permission was given, and Rose was married to Peter Scittine in 1921. The wedding took place in the Catholic church in Chicago. The reception would be long remembered by the family and friends who were there.

"Did you ever see so much food for a wedding party? It's the largest feast I've ever attended."

"It was certainly a celebration. As much whiskey as anyone wanted, and the music and dancing lasted far into the night."

One neighbor had been unable to attend. "I heard about the wonderful entertainment," she said wistfully. "There won't be another party like that around here, and I couldn't be there."

Maria missed her oldest daughter, but a new baby girl kept her occupied. Two other important events occurred that year, and one of them would change the course of the Mannoia family's life in a way that Maria never dreamed or expected.

CHAPTER THREE

TROUBLE FOLLOWS MARIA

CHICAGO SEEMED TO BE BLOWN BY THE WIND north and south along the sprawling coastline of Lake Michigan. In the early 1920s, this great metropolitan area had all the corruption that could be packed into a 200 square mile space. As a result of the passage of the 18th Amendment to the Constitution outlawing the manufacture and distribution of liquor, bootlegging activity was rampant in the city. Police officers were paid for ignoring crime in the streets. Political bosses and government officials broke the law and defrauded the people without fear of reprisal. At the same time, Chicago had the dubious pleasure of being the birthplace of the Communist Labor Party of the United States.

A few miles to the northwest of the big city, the village of Melrose Park became the new home of the Mannoias. Since the Scittine family lived there also, Maria was still close to Rose. Her joy in that fact was overshadowed when, two days after the move, her 11-month-old baby girl died of a fever. The new neighbors on 22nd Street were sympathetic and tried to comfort the family in their loss. Maria again set up an altar and prayed daily to Mary. Her pain was not eased, however, and she was glad when a neighbor woman came to call on her.

"Here, Maria, I've brought you a book."

"What is it?"

"A Bible. Read it. It will help you in your time of sorrow."

As Maria read, the Lord opened her heart and mind. Here were things she had not heard before! Surely the priest had never told her about Christ's death for *her* sins! She didn't remember hearing of God's great love and compassion for His children. In this book so new to her, she searched in vain for directions that told her to pray daily to Mary or confess her sins to the priest and accept the penance he laid out.

After several months, Maria sought out Mr. Scittine, Rose's father-in-law.

"Mr. Scittine, you have lived here for many years. Is there an evangelical church in Melrose Park?"

Startled, the old man asked, "Why are you looking for a Protestant church? You were baptized a Catholic and you will always be one."

"I want someone to explain what I read in the Bible. It tells me things I've never heard before. Why does the priest not explain about salvation and a new life?"

Mr. Scittine shrugged. "Religion is the priest's business. He tells us everything the Bible says that we need to know."

"I want to make it my business. I want to learn for myself what God says. Now, is there a church?"

"You will be sorry," Mr. Scittine predicted darkly. "This is a good Catholic community. Protestants are not well accepted here." He looked at Maria's determined face. "I see you are not convinced. There is a church on 18th Avenue."

The following day, after Vincenzo left for work and the boys for school, Maria took Annie firmly by the hand and began the walk toward a new life.

The church was easily found, and Maria learned that the man standing in front of it was the minister. Never one to waste time in trivialities, Maria came right to the point.

"Is this an evangelical church?"

The minister looked at the young woman carefully.

"Yes. Yes, it is."

"May I come to your church?"

This is not what the man expected. For a moment he was unable to reply. Then he found his voice.

"You are Italian."

"Yes. Does that make a difference?"

The minister cleared his throat and looked embarrassed. He avoided answering the question directly.

"If you are seeking a Protestant church, I believe you would be happier at the Presbyterian mission on 22nd Avenue. The minister there is Italian."

Resolutely, Maria turned back to her own street to find the mission. She soon located the place, a storefront building.

But to her disappointment, they had only Sunday school. This was better than nothing, however, and the very next Sunday morning Maria, Dominic, Joe and Annie attended the mission. When she found out about it, Rose was appalled.

"Mama! How could you attend a *Protestant* church? What will the priest say?"

"I'm not going to tell him. It's none of his business."

"Someone will tell him. Then you will be in trouble."

Maria shook her head. "There is no one who will talk. I'm the only woman who attends the mission."

"Mama! You mean just *men* go there? Whatever are you thinking? What does Papa say?"

"I haven't told him either. If I'm going to have trouble from the priest, why should I want it from your father also?"

Rose was alarmed for her mother. Nothing she said would dissuade Maria, for the longer she attended the little mission, the more she wanted to learn about God and the Bible.

Trouble, when it came, arrived from an unexpected source. Mrs. Merici, landlady of the rented house on 22nd Street, appeared at the door early one Monday morning.

"Buon giorno (good morning), Mrs. Merici. Come in, please."

"No, I will stay out here. What I have to say will not take long. I hear that you are attending a Protestant church. Is that so?"

"It is."

"Then you will have to find another place to live. We are a good Catholic neighborhood and we do not wish to have Protestants living among us."

"And is a person not free in this land to choose her own church?"

"Yes, but not in this house. You must move by the end of the month."

The matter was closed, and Mrs. Merici departed in righteous splendor. Maria shut the door slowly and sat down to think the matter through. This was a development she hadn't anticipated. Vincenzo would need to know, and how would he react? Where would she find another house in Melrose Park that they would be allowed to rent?

Leaving her new church and her search for the Lord was not an option. Therefore, Maria concluded, it was necessary for her to begin to pray directly to God and tell Him her need.

"Dear Lord, you heard what Mrs. Merici said. Now would you please give us a little house for my husband, me and our three children to live in. And help Mr. Mannoia to understand why we have to move. Thank you. Oh, yes and give me a house — even if it is on the alley."

Maria went back to her work, singing as she always did, and waited for the Lord to answer her prayer. She didn't wait long. Later that day, another visitor appeared at the door. It was Mr. Scittine.

"Come in, come in. I have fresh rolls and coffee."

"Are you still attending your Protestant church, Mrs. Mannoia?"

"Yes, Mr. Scittine. Every Sunday."

"And what does Mr. Mannoia say?"

"Tonight we will see." Maria related what the landlady had told her that morning.

"So, would you like to buy a house?"

"Yes, Mr. Scittine, I certainly need one. But I don't have that much money."

"How much do you have?"

"Five hundred dollars."

Mr. Scittine said, "That will do. The house is larger than this one. It's on 21st Avenue. We will go see it in the morning." He arose to leave, then thought of something else. "Of course, this house is on the alley."

"That's all right, Mr. Scittine. I told Him I would live on an alley."

"Told him? You talked with someone about a house before I got here? Who did you talk to?"

"The Lord. I told Him I needed a place to live, and because I didn't request a large and beautiful home, He has provided just what we need. Thank you, Mr. Scittine."

He shook his head as he went out the door. "Trouble," he muttered to himself. "I see trouble ahead."

It was just as well that he did not see it when it came,

for Vincenzo was furious when Maria told him that they would have to leave the rented house.

"Mrs. Merici doesn't like the church I attend," Maria explained.

"Why? What does she have against the Catholic church?"

"It's not the Catholic church. It's the Presbyterian mission."

Vincenzo was speechless. Maria continued her sewing and waited for his voice to return. When it did, the war predicted by Rose and her father-in-law began in earnest.

"You are attending the Presbyterian mission? What about your own church? You were born a Catholic! You were baptized a Catholic! Don't I have enough cares in this world without you leaving the Church and taking the children with you? Why did you do this thing?"

"I am searching for God. I want to know about the Lord for myself."

"What the priest tells you isn't good enough? You have to know more than the priest does? You have to bring ruin to our family to know more about God? Who says this to you?"

"I feel it in my heart. God is speaking to me."

"You are taking leave of your mind. You will cause trouble. Nothing but trouble."

WHEN THE FAMILY HAD FINALLY MOVED INTO the new home, Vincenzo, somewhat mollified, discovered that there was room in the yard for a garden. A glass-covered hotbed, a fig tree in the front and grapevines along the walkway were a source of satisfaction to him. Less satisfying to Maria was the winepress that Vincenzo set up in the basement.

"I have grown grapes and made my own wine all my life. Now you complain."

"I don't like it."

"Well, I don't like to pay for someone else's wine which is never as good as my own. Is this my basement? Can't I do what I want to in my own house? This I enjoy, so this I'll do."

Nevertheless, Maria was happy about the move and the permanent home the Lord had given her. Day by day her heart opened more as she joyfully obeyed all that she knew and understood about this new faith.

There was a problem about which Maria prayed and thought. In her old neighborhood in Chicago, she had felt free to call the ladies to come to her home to light the candles and pray. In this new community, she could no longer do that. Although she had not met the priest at St. Ignacius, she was well aware that word would reach him quickly if she dared to invite her neighbors in to hear about the Lord. Once again her wonderful talent as a seamstress solved the problem for her.

"Maria, *stati zitto!"* (Maria, be still!) Mrs. Amati called good naturedly over the fence as Maria hung clothes on the line and sang loudly.

"*Non posso,*" (I can't), Maria called back, "I sing because I'm happy!"

Mrs. Amati came to the fence. "What are these songs you sing?"

"Hymns, Mrs. Amati. I sing to God."

"Where did you learn them? I've never heard that music at church. Did you sing them in Sicily?"

"No, I learned them at the little mission on 22nd Street."

Mrs. Amati looked alarmed and glanced around to see if anyone else might be listening.

"The Protestant church? What will you do if anyone finds out?"

"I'll tell them about the Lord. If you come to my house, I'll tell you all about Him."

"Oh, I wouldn't dare!"

Maria regarded her thoughtfully. "Do you have any garments that need to be made over, or any sewing to be done?"

"Why, yes. But ... ?"

"Bring them. I will sew for you without cost if you will stay and listen to what God has shown me. I want people to know that the Lord has called me in this holy way."

Mrs. Amati came, and after listening to Maria's testimony and hearing verses from the Bible, she was convinced that what her neighbor told her was true. Soon Mrs. del Sarto, Mrs. Bartoli and Mrs. Luigi were also bringing mending or dresses to alter and talking together around Maria's table. They became convinced that what she told them had some merit, and one by one they began attending the Presbyterian mission together.

Eleven-year-old Dominic was not to be outdone by his mother. He was not ashamed to let the children at school know of his faith in Jesus, and soon they were coming, together with their mothers, to the Protestant mission on Sunday morning.

FATHER LEO AT ST. IGNACIUS CHURCH IN Melrose Park was puzzled. Something was going on in his parish that he didn't understand. There was an undercurrent of unrest, but he could not identify the source. The church wasn't so large that he couldn't keep track of his flock, but he had weightier matters on his mind than the activities of four or five women under his care. Nevertheless, the problems seemed to surround these ladies.

Seated in his office, Father Leo cast his mind back over the year. Had anything unusual taken place that he was overlooking? He frowned as he tried to remember what Mrs. Amati had told him several months ago. Oh, yes. He recalled the conversation.

"Father, a new family has moved here from Chicago. They are living on 22nd Avenue."

"Is that so?"

Mrs. Amati nodded. "There are three children. And I hear that they are related to the Scittines."

The conversation had been forgotten by Father Leo, but now as it came to mind, he tried to picture the new arrivals.

Surely no unknown supplicants had come to confession or he would remember them. He seemed to recall that the Scittine boy had married recently at the cathedral in Chicago. This must be the family of his bride.

The priest arose and looked out his office window. It was coming back to him now. At a later time, Mrs. Amati had imparted more news.

"The new family has bought the house next door to us, Father. Their name is Mannoia — Vincenzo and Maria."

Mannoia. He had heard that name. Almost a year ago Father Benedict had told him about Maria Mannoia.

"She is an exceptional parishioner. I understand she is an undisputed leader among the ladies in her neighborhood. Some of them who have been very remiss in church attendance have begun to come faithfully. They gather in her home to do the Novena. I would say she has brought new life to San Anselmo."

Father Leo had yet to see these people. And even more disturbing, he had not even seen Mrs. Amati, Mrs. del Sarto or Mrs. Luigi for several weeks. And who knew how many others he had lost track of? Could there be a connection between their disappearance from the church service and the new family? He would make it a point to investigate.

Consequently, Father Leo approached the elder Mr. Scittine.

"I understand some of your family has moved into the area."

"Not exactly my family, Father. They are my son's in-laws."

"I've not had the pleasure of meeting them."

Mr. Scittine was evasive. "Well, I'm sure you will soon, Father. There will be a new baby within the month, and they'll surely arrange for baptism."

Mr. Scittine was not as confident as he tried to sound. He personally had never met anyone like Maria. That she was not his wife was a relief to him. Such independence in a woman was nothing but trouble. He certainly didn't intend to share with the priest that he, Mr. Scittine, had actually directed Maria to an evangelical church!

Would Maria defy her husband and refuse to allow the child to have a Catholic baptism? Mr. Scittine dismissed the thought from his mind. She wouldn't dare. It would endanger the welfare of her own soul as well as that of her child.

Something told Mr. Scittine that Maria *could* dare to do that and very possibly would. Subsequent events proved that his fears were not unfounded. Shortly after his new son arrived, an angry Mr. Mannoia sought out his daughter's father-in-law.

"What have I done to deserve this? Why should the devil be working in my home? Eight children have been baptized in the church, and now she refuses! She will not give my son a Christian baptism in the Catholic Church! I don't remember asking for this kind of trouble!"

Mr. Scittine was not surprised. He offered a word of advice to his friend.

"If your wife will not do as you say, then you must take matters into your own hands."

"You mean knock some sense into her?"

Mr. Scittine shook his head. "No, that won't accomplish one thing. You must take the baby to the priest yourself."

"All right. Come along."

"Come? I have nothing to do with this."

"You must stand with me," Vincenzo insisted. "Maria will protest."

Reluctantly, Mr. Scittine accompanied Vincenzo to his home. Maria was hospitable, but wary.

"Please be seated, Mr. Scittine."

"No," her husband said. "He is going to accompany us to the church."

"There is no 'us.' I'm not going, and neither is the baby."

Mr. Scittine stood uneasily by the door. He had to admit a grudging respect for this little woman who stood firm in the face of her husband's rage.

"I can't carry you to the church, but I can carry my son!" Quickly Vincenzo grabbed the baby from the basket and headed for the door. As the two men left, Maria called after them.

"Do what you want. A little water won't hurt him. But when he is grown, the Lord will baptize him with the Holy Spirit and with fire."

Maria had the last word.

CHAPTER FOUR

DAYS OF HATE

MRS. DEL SARTO HANDED HER SKIRT TO MARIA then sat down and rested her arms on the kitchen table.

"My husband is not happy," she stated.

"Is that so?"

"The priest has inquired about my absence from mass. Rudy threatens to tell him that I am attending the Protestant mission."

Maria threaded new elastic into the waist band of the skirt. "I intend to tell the priest myself. The Bible says that if anyone is ashamed to confess Christ to all men, Christ will not confess them before God."

Mrs. del Sarto stared at Maria in horror. "You would tell the priest? Do you know what he will do? He will see that your life is not worth living."

"Christ said, 'In this world you will have persecution. But fear not; I have overcome the world.' If our lives are made harder, Jesus will stand with us."

It was well that Maria believed that, for the result of

her visit to the priests was harsher than she could ever have imagined. Father Leo and Father Paulo welcomed her into the parish office.

Father Leo smiled kindly. "We are glad to see you. You were not able to be present when your husband brought your son to be baptized."

"I chose not to come," Maria replied.

Father Leo's eyebrows went up, and the smile left his face as he stared at the little lady before him in surprise.

"You chose not to come to your own son's baptism into the faith? But what has happened to your devotion to the church?"

"My devotion now is to Christ."

"I'm afraid I don't understand, Mrs. Mannoia. The church worships Christ."

Maria nodded, "As best you know. But I have decided to find the Lord for myself."

"The teaching we have given you is not adequate?"

"I needed more than teaching, Father. I needed the presence of God in my life. So I have changed religions."

Father Leo asked with anger in his voice, "And I suppose you think you have found what you are looking for?"

"I still have much to learn. But I have found the eternal High Priest, the One who has purged my sins away. I find nothing in the Bible about the Purgatory you would have me believe. I have read that for the child of God who trusts in

Christ as his Savior, 'to be absent from the body is to be present with Christ.' There is no time during which someone on earth must pay money, or light candles, or pray for my soul. Christ has taken care of that with His death on the cross."

Father Leo's face turned red. Maria knew that his wrath would be vented upon her, but she had more to say.

"I do not read that I must come to you to confess my sins, Father. I don't need to give my messages to the Holy Mother. I can talk directly to my Heavenly Father and He forgives. Christ ..."

"Enough!" Father Leo thundered. "How dare you come to this holy place and utter such blasphemy! You are a disgrace to your baptism as a Catholic. You have renounced your parents and all they have taught you. What's more, you have betrayed Christ Himself! This church belongs to Christ, and if you leave the church, you leave Christ."

Father Leo stopped for breath, and Father Paulo took up the tirade. "You will spend eternity in hell for this dissension, Mrs. Mannoia. Unless you confess and return to the fold, you have committed a mortal sin against God and the church."

Maria had not finished with the subject, though she knew that pursuing it further would bring deeper trouble to her.

"I can show you in the Holy Word of God that what I say is true. I have the witness of the Spirit in my heart that tells me that I have not made a mistake." She looked steadily at the two furious priests in front of her. "Can you show me in God's Word that what the church has taught me is really true?"

There was silence in the room for a long moment. Then Father Leo arose and leaned across his desk. His voice shook with anger. "You would challenge the ones God has set over you as shepherds? You would call us teachers of false doctrine? You would blaspheme our Lord in this holy place?"

"The *Lord* is my shepherd, Father. He has said 'Come unto *Me,* all you who are heavy laden.' He said, '*My* sheep know *My* voice.' I choose to believe Him over what mortal man can tell me."

Father Leo straightened up and pointed toward the door. "Go, Mrs. Mannoia. You are not worthy to be on the holy grounds of this church. You are an infidel of the worst kind, and you have not heard the last of this. You will live to regret this heresy."

Maria walked home with joy in her heart and a smile on her face. The Lord had given her the victory! With every step she praised God for the new understanding she had, and for the courage He had given her to face the priests with her testimony. Regret it? Never! The devil and all his angels could not cause her to fear or to back down. The Lord was her strength and her shield. In Him was her trust. Together they would face whatever came.

As busy as she was in the next few days, Maria could not help but be aware of a change in the neighborhood. When she walked to the market, the ladies who usually stopped to talk with her waved and hurried on. Those who stood in their yards nodded in her direction, then ducked into the house. No one brought sewing or came to hear the Bible read. Maria was puzzled. Had she done something to offend them?

At the end of the week, the mystery was solved. The boys came in from school, and as they munched warm cookies, Joe watched his mother working at the stove.

"Mama, did you buy this house for us?"

"Joe!" Dominic gave him a warning poke, but his younger brother wouldn't be silenced.

"Yes," Maria said, "I bought the house. It belongs to us."

"Then why do we have to move away from here?"

"You and your big mouth," Dominic said in disgust. "Now you've done it."

Maria sat down and looked from one boy to the other. "So, what is it?"

"Aw, he's just listening to the kids at school. They don't like it that we attend the Protestant mission."

"They push us off the sidewalk," Joe added. "They said the priest told them to."

"Jesus said, 'Blessed are you when men persecute you … for my sake, … for great will be your reward in heaven.' We will pray for them."

When she saw Mrs. Amati in the yard next door, Maria went out to the fence.

"Lucy, I need to talk with you." Reluctantly her neighbor approached the fence.

"What is going on that I don't know about? I'm sure it has something to do with me. What is it?"

Mrs. Amati looked distressed, and she started to say, "It's nothing, Maria," but she changed her mind. "I can't talk now," she said. "We will be over this evening after dark. We will talk then."

It was a solemn group of ladies who gathered around the kitchen table that night. "We have not dared come to see you or talk to you on the street during the day for fear the priests would see us," Mrs. del Sarto confided.

"The priests have told you not to speak to me? Is it because I attend a Protestant church?"

They nodded.

"But you attend with me on Sunday night. What do they say about that?"

"We haven't told them," Mrs. Bartoli admitted. "And we would never dare to argue with them as you did!"

"I didn't argue. I simply stated the truth and *they* argued. Is it better to obey men or God?"

"But Maria, aren't you afraid of what will happen?"

"'I will not fear what men shall do unto me.' The Lord is with me. What can happen?"

The ladies looked at each other helplessly, then Lucy Amati spoke for them.

"It has already happened, Maria. The priest has ordered that every Catholic family on the street must sign a petition to have you move away. They will go from house to house to collect names saying that they do not want Protestants on their street. When the sheets of paper have been filled, they will take it to court to ask the judge to force you to leave. We can do nothing to stop it."

Maria considered this news carefully. "Then that means you can no longer be my friends?"

"We *will* be your friends," Mrs. Bartoli said. "We will continue to come at night for Bible studies, no matter where you are. We want to learn more about a Lord who makes you strong enough to defy the priests!"

"I will be right here," Maria told them. "God gave me this house for my family, and He will not allow the priest to take it away from me. We will continue to read God's Word and learn from it."

In the days that followed, it seemed that what the priests could not forcefully remove, the courts might decide. Maria received notice that the case had been taken to law, and her presence would be required to testify.

IT SEEMED TO FATHER LEO THAT HE HAD SPENT an inordinate amount of time pacing his office floor in recent weeks. He could not recall any time in his years in the pastorate that there had been so much uneasiness in his parish. Melrose

Park was predominantly Italian and Catholic. There were Protestants there, to be sure, but they were of no concern to him. He supposed that they attended their own churches and minded their own business. He had no disagreement with them until now.

When a life-long, born-in-the-faith Catholic decided to join with Protestants, and (he was sure) persuade several friends to go with her, it was his duty to take action. This had been done, and now the letter informing him of the court date for this matter lay on his desk. The letter was not addressed to him but had been relayed to him by a loyal parishioner.

Although Father Leo had instigated the plot to remove Maria Mannoia and family from the neighborhood, he well knew that bringing action in the court against them in the name of the church would only arouse dissension in the community. For the same reason, he could not be seen attending the hearing. Father Paulo was equally well known and must not risk being found there. Father Leo concluded that he would be obliged to recruit a young student from a nearby parish to sit in the courtroom and report back to him.

On the day of the hearing, Maria took Anne and Jimmy to stay with Rose. "What do you have to do, Mama?"

"Testify. I'll tell the judge what the Lord has done for me."

Rose looked doubtful. "I don't think that's what they'll be talking about. Are you sure you don't have to tell him why you should stay in your house?"

"Of course! I'll say that God gave me this house, and

until He takes it away from me, I will continue to live here."

"Mama, what else are you going to say to the judge?" Rose regarded her mother suspiciously. "Are you planning to preach to him?"

"Certainly not! I will just testify about God's grace. The devil seeks to get the best of me, but he can do nothing. The Lord has given me all the armor I need so that I can stand straight on my feet. I will praise the Lord in all my times, and His praise shall continually be in my mouth! Glory to His holy and blessed name!"

Rose sighed. "That's just what I thought. You're going to preach to him. I hope he doesn't put you in jail."

"Paul went to jail. I can testify there too. I must go now."

By the time the court appearance was over, the young student, like one of the wise men, was sorely tempted to return home by another way. Father Leo, however, knew where to find him, so reluctantly he turned his steps toward the church and the waiting priest. Carefully he recounted all that had been said in court. Father Leo listened with growing alarm.

"And the outcome?"

"The judge told the people who brought the papers that if they continue to disturb Mrs. Mannoia, he would put them in jail."

The priest groaned and held his head.

"Did she mention my name?"

"No, Father."

"Did she blaspheme the church?"

"No, Father."

Father Leo stared into space for a long moment. The young man shifted uncomfortably in his seat, well aware of the fate of a messenger when the message was unacceptable. He was greatly relieved when the priest rose to dismiss him.

"She has not heard the last of this yet. We are not finished with her," Father Leo said. "You may go."

For Maria, the outcome of the hearing was exactly what she had expected. The Lord had upheld her, and she had testified to the judge, even though the lawyer had tried to stop her.

"I was called to testify and I'm going to testify for my Lord," she declared.

The judge was kind enough to permit her to continue. She wasn't surprised that he had ruled in her favor. The brush with the church and the law was of little consequence to her, but breaking the news to her parents would bring real sorrow to her heart.

IN MISILMERI, MAMA HOVERED ANXIOUSLY around the door, occasionally walking out and looking up the cobbled street toward town.

"What could be keeping her?" she muttered. "All she had to do was pick up the mail. It couldn't take this long."

"Mama you are talking about *Anita,*" Josephine said. "You know she can't walk that far without stopping to talk to her friends. Just hope she remembers that she went for the mail."

Mama didn't listen. "Can you believe that Maria and

Rosalina have new babies just two months apart? Almost 10 years they have been gone, and I've not seen any of the babies. How could they ..."

"Here she comes, Mama," Josephine interrupted her, "and she does have a handful of mail."

"A big letter from Maria, Mama," Anita called. "Hurry and tell us what she says about Jimmy and baby Rosie."

Mama snatched the envelope and opened it quickly. Suddenly her face turned white, and the pages slipped from her hands to the floor.

The girls looked at her in horror.

"Mama! What is the matter with Maria? Is she dead?"

"Yes."

Josephine picked up a page from the floor.

"She can't be dead, Mama. She wrote the letter!"

"She is dead. We will talk of it when your father gets home."

Josephine read the sheet she was holding.

"For a long time," Maria wrote, "I have been longing to know Jesus as my Savior and Redeemer. Since I've searched the scripture, I've found the Word of Life. The Lord is my Light and my Salvation. I have come to believe that I can no longer be a Catholic, for I have found a better way. I pray that my beloved parents and sisters will also search and find the true Savior."

"Oh, no!" Josephine gasped. "How could she do this? She will lose her soul!"

Late into the night her family mourned for Maria. The following day a letter was dispatched to America.

"As far as we are concerned, we do not have a daughter Maria. Since our former daughter has made the decision to leave her home, her family and her Church, we are no longer willing to correspond with her."

Maria reported this news to Rose.

"'When my father and my mother forsake me, then the Lord will take me up,'" she said.

"I couldn't stand it to lose my mama and papa like that." Rose hugged her little Rosie to her. "I know I'd never be able to reject my child. Are you sure it's worth it, Mama?"

"Worth it? Thanks be to God who gave His only Son to die for me!" Tears ran down Maria's face. "Jesus said that 'Whoever loves mother or father more than me is not worthy of me.' And I want to be worthy of Him! If I were younger, I'd go back and talk to them personally. I'm sure they would listen to me."

Maria looked thoughtfully at the letter.

"I can't go to Sicily, but I can go to New York and witness to my brother and his family. They will hear what I say. And I can still write my sisters. I won't give up!"

In spite of her prayers and her best efforts, Maria was rejected by her brother. In return for the tracts she sent to her sisters, they sent pictures of Mary and the saints. Their hearts were not open to the Lord. Although this was a source of sorrow for Maria, it did not sway her dedication to the Lord or her new belief.

CHAPTER FIVE

GOD HAS A PLAN

THE WIND WHISTLED AROUND THE CORNERS OF the buildings, and Maria pulled her coat tightly across her shoulders. Walking would be easier if she could turn and go the other way, she thought, but that wouldn't lead toward home. As she pondered the idea, she realized that this was true of her Christian life, too. The easy road led away from her goal — that everyone in Melrose Park should know about her God. This day had not been filled with success.

The events of the day might not have seemed so overwhelming had they not all happened at once.

Rose had offered to keep Annie and the baby while Maria did her errands.

"It's much too cold to take them with you. I'll stay here until you come back. You don't want to be out there too long yourself on a day like this."

Maria headed toward the store. She would call on a neighbor or two along the way. She had not visited Mrs. Magnini in her home, but they had spoken when they met on the street.

At Maria's knock, the door opened a crack and Mrs. Magnini peered out. "I can't ask you to come in, Mrs. Mannoia. You'll have to leave."

"Do you have illness?"

"No, no." Mrs. Magnini thrust out her head and looked cautiously at the street. "The priest has ordered us not to speak to you," she whispered. "We must not let you in the house. I'm sorry."

The door clicked shut and Maria turned away. So, Father Leo had not forgotten the court hearing. If he couldn't force her to leave the neighborhood, he would see that she had no one to talk with. Never mind. She wasn't afraid of what the priest could do. The Lord was with her, and her experiences made her stronger.

At the next house Mrs. Lucci's husband was at home. "I'll thank you to stay away from my house," he shouted. "You do nothing but upset my wife. She thinks about leaving the church like you have. The devil take you and your heresy!"

The store wasn't crowded, but the owner's wife was nervous as she waited on Maria. "If any of the women think I'm talking to you about anything but business, they'll go straight to the priest. So we can't visit."

"That's all right, Julie. I understand. The ladies are still coming to my house in the evening to hear the Bible. You come. There we can talk."

The woman nodded, and Maria took her bag and

stepped out in the cold again. "Thy rod and thy staff, they comfort me. Thou preparest a table before me in the presence of mine enemies. My cup runneth over ..." David must have known what it felt like to be rejected, yet he could say, "The *Lord* is my shepherd ..." Maria pondered these things as she turned toward home. How grateful she was for the little mission that had taken them in. The Lord was good.

All that had been half an hour ago, Maria thought as she struggled against the wind. In spite of herself she had to smile as she thought how appropriate that Scripture had been in the light of what happened next. The Lord had saved the worst for the last. A voice behind Maria had called to her.

"Mrs. Mannoia! Mrs. Mannoia! Can you come in for a minute?"

It was the pastor of the Presbyterian mission. The small office into which he ushered her was warmer than the outdoors, but he wore a heavy sweater. As he bustled about preparing a cup of tea for her, he talked nervously.

"I'm glad I saw you going by. I've been planning to get over to visit you very soon. Sugar in your tea? Cream? No? Well, it is hot. It will take the chill off. This is a wild day to be out, isn't it? But then, one must have groceries."

Finally he sat down behind his desk and regarded Maria anxiously.

"Mrs. Mannoia, I have bad news for you. I really would rather not tell you, but you will have to know right away. It has been a privilege to be your pastor. I have been blessed to minister to you and the ladies who come with you."

Maria's heart sank as she asked, "Are you leaving?"

"The mission is closing, Mrs. Mannoia. The church can't afford to support a minister any longer. I will be assigned to another place by the end of the month."

"What will we do? We will be like a sheep without a shepherd." Even as she spoke, Maria remembered the verse that had come to her mind just as the pastor called to her. "The *Lord* is my shepherd ..."

The minister was answering her. "The Lord has great plans for you, Mrs. Mannoia. He is not going to depart from you or leave you without a place to worship. There are other evangelical churches in this area, and you must pray for direction to find the one God has for you."

Maria hurried as quickly as she could when she started for home again. The boys would be there soon — perhaps they were there already. The boys. How could she tell them that their church had closed and they had nowhere to go?

"Don't worry, Mama," Dominic told her. "My friends and I know about another church. It's on 15th Avenue, and they will be glad to have us."

"It has to be a spiritual church," Maria said. "It must help us to know God better. We still have a lot to learn. What is it called?"

"It's a Free Methodist church, Mama. Their pastor has

visited the mission several times. My friends Joe and Jimmy and I have gone there on Sunday evening."

SEVERAL MONTHS LATER THE CHURCH BELL RANG early on Saturday morning, startling the neighbors surrounding the little Free Methodist church on 15th Avenue.

"What's going on over there? A wedding?"

"No, they don't ring the bell for weddings. Must be a funeral."

"We'd have heard if someone died. The preacher must think this is Sunday."

Something unusual was occurring, but it was none of the events the neighbors were suggesting.

The District Quarterly Meeting was regularly held in one of the churches of the Illinois Conference, under the direction of the district elder. Because of its size and location in the midst of a predominantly Catholic community, Melrose Park did not often host the quarterly meeting. Today, however, was an exception.

The decision had been made some time before when Pastor Simon had consulted with the elder, Brother Hall.

"I've been watching your monthly reports with great interest, Brother Simon. I am curious to know what is going on in Melrose Park. Where are all the people coming from? I'm surprised that you could report an increase of over 50 people in attendance since the last quarterly meeting. Is it possible that your preaching has improved that much since I last heard you?" He chuckled at his own humor, and the pastor smiled with him.

"I wish I could say that you guessed right, but the truth is that a majority of the new attendees don't even understand English. God is working in their hearts in an unusual way. Let me tell you about it."

Brother Hall settled back in his chair and listened as Pastor Simon related what had happened in Melrose Park.

"One Sunday morning a few months ago, three young boys from the community attended Sunday school. I had seen them before at the Italian Presbyterian mission, and supposed they were just visiting that day. To my surprise, they returned the following Sunday, and with them 31 more people — young and old! That evening, everyone returned."

The elder interrupted him.

"But you say most of them didn't understand English? How did you communicate with them?"

"God communicated with them, Brother Hall. I soon discovered that the leader of the group was a little lady by the name of Maria Mannoia. She and the ladies who come with her left the Catholic Church in order to learn about God for themselves. Her oldest son, Dominic, told me that his mother had Bible studies daily with any ladies who would come to her home. She had studied on her own, and the Holy Spirit had revealed the Word to her heart."

"Remarkable! And have you seen spiritual development among them?"

"Yes indeed. Just a few weeks ago, Mrs. Mannoia accepted the Lord as her Savior. In speaking with Dominic, I believe she understands the step she has taken and is anxious to grow in grace. She says she has no desire for the Catholic religion. She has been given a new birth."

"And what do you foresee as the future of this group, Brother Simon?"

"I believe they need a place of their own to worship and an Italian minister."

Brother Hall nodded. "We will hold the next quarterly session in Melrose Park. This matter must have careful consideration."

OLD MR. MARINI REMOVED THE "FOR RENT" sign from his building on 24th Avenue and Lake Street and dumped it into the trash bin. Louisa would be happy to know that they would be receiving $50 a month for the room. Fortunately, Louisa didn't get down here often. He wouldn't bother to tell her who the new renters were. In truth, he had been reluctant to accept the offer himself when he learned what was going on there.

The man who inquired seemed pleased with the size of the building and the rent.

"This should be adequate," he said. "It will hold 50 or 60 people."

"Depends on what they're planning to do," Mr. Marini said. "Not enough room for that many to dance."

"They won't be dancing. This will be a mission."

"You mean a church house?"

"That's right. A group of Italian Protestants will be worshiping here."

Mr. Marini shook his head. "You're asking for trouble, Mr. Simon. This is a good Catholic neighborhood. When folks find out what's going on here, they'll run them out."

The vision of anyone running Maria Mannoia out of anywhere amused Pastor Simon.

"We'll take that chance, Mr. Marini."

The Italian members were pleased with their own building and promise of an Italian pastor. Other families came, and the group increased. True to Mr. Marini's prediction, the Catholic neighbors soon found out what was taking place at 24th and Lake Street.

"The devil is suggesting ways for them to get rid of us," Maria said. "But never mind. We will prevail. The Bible says 'Resist the devil and he will flee from you.' I don't like to see so much hatred among our own Italian people, but God will see that His children are triumphant."

So when stones were thrown against the door, or objects were hurled into the building during their services, the faithful Christians continued to sing and pray and read the Bible. Spiteful actions did not deter them, and Maria was happy to report to Pastor Simon.

"The Lord is with us, and through Him we are overcoming. He is adding to our number."

"FORTY-FOUR, 45, 46. THAT'S IT MAMA. That's all we have."

"Count it again, Dominic. We have to pay the rent this week."

"I've counted twice. There just isn't any more."

Maria went on with her work, but as she washed, she talked to her constant Companion.

"You know we need the money for our mission rent, Lord. The devil would be glad to see us close and have nowhere to worship. But You have told us to spread Your name in Melrose Park, and we aren't going to give up. Please show me what I need to do now."

As soon as the clean laundry was flapping from the clothesline, Maria put on her coat, bundled up Anne and Jimmy and made her way to the Free Methodist church. She lost no time in putting the problem before Pastor Simon.

"It is becoming harder each month to pay the $50 rent for our building," she told him. "We are four dollars short this month. Mr. Marini would be glad to see us gone, and so would the devil. But I believe God has a plan for us."

"We can help you with the rent this month," the pastor offered, "but that isn't a good solution for the future."

Maria nodded. "I believe the Lord is directing us to

have our own house of worship. If we owned two lots, we could build a small church. I would like permission to look for a property."

Pastor was well aware of the business ability this lady possessed. He also knew she was open to the Lord's direction in an unusual way.

"I agree that your congregation needs a better place to worship. You have my permission to search for two lots. When you have found them, we will talk about the next step."

Maria praised the Lord for His leading as she walked toward home. There was no doubt in her mind that He would show her the lots they should have. Undoubtedly she had passed them many times as she called from house to house in the village. In the morning she would begin to look.

Suddenly, she stopped in her tracks. There they were — just five blocks from the Free Methodist church on 20th Avenue. Maria stared at the lots in amazement, then turned and looked across the street. She was directly in front of the alley that led to her house on 21st Avenue! Anne had run ahead of her mother, but now she came back and tugged at her skirt.

"Why are you looking at that empty field, Mama? What do you see?"

"A church, Annie. I see a church."

Anne was puzzled. "I don't see it, Mama."

"You will, daughter. God has promised us one."

Plans moved forward quickly. It took a long time to

locate the owner of the property, but Maria succeeded. Mr. Thornton listened to her request to purchase the two lots on 20th Avenue.

"Yeah, I could sell 'em. It'll cost ya $1,500."

"This property will belong to the Lord," she told him. "He showed me where to find them. There will be a church here, and it will be dedicated to God."

"Yeah? Well, it'll still cost ya $1,500. When I see the money, ya get the deed."

"I want to invite you to attend the services, Mr. Thornton. Jesus Christ died for your soul, and you need to come and hear about His love for you. We'll be meeting on Sunday morning and evening and Wednesday night. Oh, yes — Sunday school, too. You need to study the Bible."

Mr. Thornton watched in amazement as Maria walked away, then he turned and looked at the empty lots.

"She talks like the church was already standing there," he muttered to himself. "She could make a believer out of me!"

Pastor Simon was happy to tell Maria and the congregation that the General Missionary Board was willing to assist the Italian mission in purchasing the property. This was not a surprise to Maria. "You saw how the Lord directed me to the lots," she said. "Would He do that if He didn't intend for us to have a mission of our own soon? We will pray now about the building."

Maria not only prayed; she expected a church. Money

would be needed to build on the lots, she thought. However, the Lord had another plan, one which advertised the new mission better than they could have imagined.

Dominic came in from school with an announcement.

"Mama, remember that big garage over on 15th Avenue, right near the Free Methodist church? It's for sale."

"Yes?"

"It's too bad it's so far away from our new lots. It's big enough for a church."

Maria thought that over as she prepared dinner. It wouldn't hurt to go look at it in the morning. With God nothing was impossible. She would pray about it.

The following morning she made her way to the big building on 15th Avenue. Dominic had been right. It was big enough for a church. In addition, she discovered that there were five rooms upstairs. Although she had no idea how they would get the garage and the lots together, Maria knew that God would have a way. She was sure this was an answer to their prayers.

The owner, when she found him, listened with disbelief as this little lady inquired about buying his building for the Lord.

"No offense, Ma'am, but what does He need it for?"

"A church. We have a lot over on 20th Avenue, and this garage will do fine. We can rent the upstairs apartment. I believe the Lord brought this to our attention because He wants us to have it. How much are you asking for it?"

"$500, Ma'am. And if you'll pardon my inquiring, is the Lord going to move it for you?"

"Why, of course! He wouldn't give us a church if He didn't have a plan for putting it where it belonged! I'll talk to my pastor, and we'll make arrangements for the sale."

The bemused garage owner reported this unusual conversation to his wife.

"She says her name is Maria Mannoia. Either she's ready to be committed or she knows something about God that I don't know!"

"She knows about God, all right," his wife replied. "She's visited every house on this street at one time or another. It doesn't discourage her if you close the door in her face; she comes back later to see if you've changed your mind. I'm sure she *does* know more about God than we do."

CHAPTER SIX

THERE COMES TROUBLE

"LITTLE ITALY" IN MELROSE PARK WAS DEFINED as the streets included between 20th and 25th Avenues. Families who lived there were bound together by language, culture and religion. It was safe to say that Maria Mannoia had visited every home contained within those boundaries and had been met with varying degrees of acceptance or rejection.

Although Maria never missed an opportunity to tell what the Lord had done for her, or to urge those she met to "believe on the Lord Jesus Christ and be saved," her interest in her neighbors extended to a real concern and compassion for their welfare. They were not unaware of this genuineness. Maria was never too busy to stop and listen to their troubles. She was first to call when illness struck. Many babies came into the world with her able assistance. Meals were shared, necessities were provided from her small supply, and no one who needed help was turned away.

However, there was one thing that caused her neighbors to say, "Oh, oh. There comes trouble," when Maria appeared. She had left the Catholic Church, and she was not shy about urging others to do the same. Her earnest search for a life in Christ was not deterred by anything that could be said or done to her.

Rose was the most concerned for her mother's welfare.

"Mama, how can you stand to hear people say the things they do against you?"

"The Bible says, 'Count it all joy ...,' so that's what I do. I am seeking the Lord, and God says, "If you seek me with your whole heart, I will be found.' That's more important than what someone says. And see how many families are attending the mission, even without a full-time pastor! The Lord is good to us, and our numbers are increasing."

It was a tribute to Maria's leadership, then, when in early spring 1925, an unusual event took place in Little Italy.

The residents along 20th Avenue awakened to a low rumble that sounded like thunder and caused the ground to shake. Curious faces appeared at the windows, and one by one families gathered at the curbs to watch in amazement. A huge two story building, balanced on heavy beams and carried along on wheels, trundled down the center of 20th Avenue. Much to their disappointment, school didn't close for this show, so the children had to depart before the journey ended. The women continued to monitor the progress of the building until it reached the empty lots across from the alley. "I heard they were going to have a church over there, but I thought they'd build it, not bring it in already done."

"Did you ever see the like? What do you suppose Father Leo will say when he finds out about it?"

Five blocks away, Father Leo had already found out and had already spoken.

"Can you imagine the audacity of that woman, daring to put a Protestant Italian mission just five blocks from the church? Why were we not informed that this was going to happen before the lots were sold?"

"We don't know *positively* that this mission was Mrs. Mannoia's doing. I've heard that the leaders of the Free Methodist Church funded the project."

Father Leo glared at Father Paulo.

"Has anyone opened a mission in this area before that woman came?"

"No, Father."

"Has anyone else gone door-to-door to tell our members that the teaching we have given them is false?"

"No, Father."

"And who else do you know who would have the unmitigated gall to claim more knowledge of the Bible than we have?"

"No one, Father."

Father Leo sagged into the chair and mopped his forehead.

"She *must* be stopped. She is causing nothing but trouble in this community."

Had Father Leo known what lay ahead next for the village, his distress would have heightened.

LUCY AMATI STOOD ON A CHAIR IN MARIA'S kitchen and turned slowly as the hem was pinned in her new dress.

"I still can't believe that a building that big could be moved over here from 15th Avenue, Maria. Nothing like that has ever happened on this street before."

Maria nodded. "Pastor Simon arranged for Brother Howard to do it. He's a moving contractor from Evanston. We couldn't afford to hire someone who would charge full price."

She inserted the last pin in the hem.

"You can get down now. The Bible says, 'a workman is worthy of his hire.' I've been thinking that we need to help Brother Howard with that expense."

Mrs. Amati looked doubtful. "You're right, of course, but we don't receive enough in our offerings to take any out."

"Everyone needs to feel a responsibility for the new church, so we should have special offerings. But I feel led to ask the community to help us."

"The community! You mean the village of Melrose Park? The same people who throw rocks at our doors and try to break up our services?"

"Not the neighborhood families. I have thought to approach the business people. There are many who donate to projects and improvements."

Mrs. Amati shook her head in wonder.

"I can't believe you'd think something like that! This is

a *Protestant* church you're talking about. Do you think the merchants in Little Italy, or anywhere in Melrose Park would dare to give a donation to *us?*"

"We won't know until we try. I feel in my heart that I need to do this to help the Lord's work."

Lucy Amati knew better than to contend with Maria Mannoia in matters of direction from the Lord. She returned home, promising to pray about the matter, but with little hope that her friend would receive donations of much more than curses and criticism.

To just about everyone's surprise except Maria's, the campaign was successful.

"The storekeepers responded very well," Maria announced to Rose and the boys. "I told them what the money was for, and they gave me something. Some gave more than others, but always something. The Lord is to be praised for His goodness. He has promised that we would not want for any good thing, and that He will be with us in the presence of our enemies."

"Didn't anyone turn you away, Mama?" Dominic wanted to know.

"Well, yes. When I came to Marsicano's Pharmacy on Lake Street, he chased me out. He said I had shamed the Italian colony and turned the village upside down. But that's all right. Paul was told that, too. It didn't stop him and it won't stop me. The Lord is with me."

The new church was under the care of Pastor Simon, and he was quick to appoint Maria treasurer of the mission as well as overseer of the property. When the five-room apartment above the sanctuary was prepared, she leased it and collected the rent. She and the other members of the mission watched with anticipation as the building was refurbished and made ready for a house of worship. Maria spent her time calling on Italian families, and together with Dominic, continued to urge them to attend the services. No one who met her came away without hearing what the Lord had done for Maria Mannoia.

VINCENZO MANNOIA SAT ON THE PORCH OF HIS bungalow and noted with satisfaction that the new plants in the garden were doing well. His yard and grape vines gave him great pleasure. These were activities he could enjoy in any language.

Vincenzo didn't talk a lot. It was difficult for him to communicate in English, and he had become accustomed to allowing his children and Maria to take care of any English speaking that was done. Of course, Maria wasn't greatly proficient in this new language, but it certainly didn't stop her from talking to everyone she met. Many times, he had noted, it brought them nothing but trouble.

Still, Vincenzo reflected as he watched the birds hopping around the garden that he was proud of Maria. She was an excellent business woman — thrifty and knowledgeable about finances. What she could do with a few dollars!

Vincenzo glanced down the alley towards the lots on 20th Avenue. Work was progressing on the new Italian mission. It would not have been possible without Maria's leadership. He rubbed his head and sighed deeply. He had never been a church man himself, but when he did attend, it was the church of his birth that he went to. So what had Maria done? Turned the village on its ear by gathering people to form a *Protestant* church!

Vincenzo had attended a few times and sat in the family pew, listening quietly. He had not yet seen the necessity for devoting his entire life to the cause, as Maria did. And he certainly had not seen the urgency to get rid of the winepress in his basement as she insisted! It seemed that lately he had heard more about that, but he wasn't ready to leave all of his past behind him.

Suddenly he was aware of a cat sunning itself on the warm glass of the hotbed.

"Scat! Get away! Out of my garden!"

Joe came to the door. "Papa, how come you holler at the cat in English, but you holler at us in Italian?"

"Cat doesn't understand Italian," Vincenzo told him.

"Sometimes I wish I didn't," Joe muttered, and went back into the house, leaving his father to ponder the events of the week ahead of him.

SUNDAY MORNING, MAY 10, 1925, WAS A pleasant day in Melrose Park, and a day of great rejoicing for the Italian mission. Neighbors along 20th Avenue had become accustomed to new and sometimes strange happenings in this Protestant church, but they were not prepared for its dedication. Having never witnessed such an event, it was doubtful that any of them had any idea what a festive atmosphere would prevail.

In the Mannoia household everyone was hurrying or being hurried. It was important that as hosts for the day they be on hand to greet the first arrivals. This would not be a gathering of five or six families and their Sunday school children. To celebrate what the Lord had done on their behalf, all the Free Methodists within traveling distance had been invited. The entire Free Methodist congregation of the 15th Avenue Church was expected as well as general officers from Headquarters.

And come they did. Maria beamed as she moved from one group to another, welcoming friends and strangers alike. All were pleased to have a fine Free Methodist Italian mission. Tears of joy were shed as the new mission was dedicated to the task of spreading the Word of God, not only in Little Italy, but in the village of Melrose Park. A special joy to Maria was the attendance of all her family, including Papa. He might never be a dynamic, outspoken Christian, she thought, but God was speaking to his heart, and she believed that Vincenzo would grow in his spiritual life. Even now he prayed before meals and listened with tears in his eyes as she read the Bible to the children.

When the day ended, Maria again praised the Lord. She and the boys sat at the kitchen table and counted the offering.

"Two thousand dollars, Mama! I can't believe we have that much money for the church!" Joe's eyes were big as he looked at the bills and coins in front of them.

"I can believe it," Maria said. "This is the Lord's work, and He has promised to bless us if we honor Him. He has surely blessed us today!"

AS THE MONTHS WENT BY AND MARIA STUDIED the Bible diligently, changes began to take place in her life. She shared her discoveries with Rose and the friends who came frequently to hear the Scriptures and pray with her.

"In Sicily we began drinking wine with our meals when we were young. Now I have read the words of Paul that say do not be drunk with wine but be filled with the Spirit," she told them. "I'll no longer drink wine."

This was not the only area of her life that changed. Maria appreciated beautiful clothes. She was aware of the latest fashions and fabrics, for she studied them carefully. Her finest work appeared in exclusive shops in Chicago, and she was in demand to produce the latest styles for friends and neighbors. As much as she loved soft silks, satins and decorative trimmings that were popular with women, Maria believed that these things were no longer acceptable for her.

If anyone ridiculed Maria's plain dresses, made from sturdy fabrics, it didn't faze her. Her clothing was as carefully crafted as any she sold to the stores, and the joy on her face far outshone the jewelry and trimmings that "the world" found so appealing.

"The Bible says that women should dress modestly and put off gold, silver and extra trimmings. Our adornment should be a meek and quiet spirit."

"There's nothing meek about you, Mama," Rose told her.

"Never mind. The Lord says that we must speak with boldness against sin. My heart is meek before the Lord."

Indeed it was. Through prayer and reading her Bible faithfully, Maria was led into a deeper experience with the Lord. She truly believed that "having the mind of Christ" was her goal, for she said, "Without holiness none can see God."

It was a happy day for the Italian mission when newly-ordained Brother Angelo came to be a full-time pastor. The faithful members of the mission were greatly encouraged by services conducted in Italian, and Maria continued to call door-to-door in the neighborhood. Some of her friends were skeptical.

"Maria, how can you stand to have people slam doors in your face and call you names? Doesn't it hurt your feelings?"

Maria was surprised. "It is God they are cursing, not me. I can't be hurt by what they say, because I'm doing what God tells me to do. Besides, you have seen that some who turned me away at first have started to attend."

"Only to get rid of you — like the story from the Bible you read to us about the wicked judge."

Maria shrugged. "Whatever. They are now hearing the Word, and the seed is sown. God will bring in the harvest."

CHAPTER SEVEN

THEY ALL MUST KNOW

MARIA ROCKED SLOWLY AS SHE READ HER BIBLE, then paused to think back over her six years in Melrose Park and her new walk with the Lord. Her heart overflowed with praise as she thought of all He had done for her.

"For I reckon that the sufferings of this present time *are* not worthy *to be compared* with the glory which shall be revealed in us" (Romans 8:18, KJV).

Maria knew that in the neighborhood she was regarded with a mixture of acceptance and hostility. She was persecuted for her religious beliefs and pushed off when she tried to share God's love. On the other hand, those who were ill or in trouble turned quickly to Maria to minister to them and pray for them. She never turned anyone away.

Only last evening, Mrs. Lucci, who lived near the Presbyterian mission, appeared at her door.

"Oh, Mrs. Mannoia," she sobbed, "I know my husband cursed at you and wouldn't let you on our porch, but we are in terrible trouble! Can you help us?"

"Come in, come in. What is it?"

"Evalyn. Our daughter Evalyn. She has run off again, and this time we can't find her. The police haven't brought her back. We lock her in her room, but she manages to get out. Always at night she leaves. I believe the devil has her soul." Mrs. Lucci continued to sob and wring her hands, "Please, can you help us?"

Maria took her coat from the peg by the door.

"Of course. Come, we'll find her. The Lord will keep her safe."

Evalyn was found, and Maria accompanied the mother and daughter to their home. Mr. Lucci glared at Maria but allowed her to enter the house.

"The devil will not have this girl," Maria declared. "The Bible says, 'Rebuke the devil and he will flee from you.' The devil cannot prevail over the forces of good. Principalities or powers will not be able to separate us from the love of God. Are you willing to pray that the Lord will take care of the evil one and heal Evalyn?"

"Oh, yes! Please pray, Mrs. Mannoia."

Maria prayed, and God answered. The girl became calm and went willingly to bed.

In the past month there had been several babies who needed healing. Baby Lydia had been born blind, and the Lord had opened her eyes in answer to prayer.

Maria's reputation as a woman who had the gift of healing spread quickly throughout the village. She wasted no time in making sure that God received the glory. To each mother, she gave a Bible.

"Read this, for in it you will find the words of life. God alone is worthy of your praise. I cannot touch your children and heal them. God heals according to His will when we pray in faith, believing."

Maria picked up her own Bible again and continued reading. With all the children in school now and a new baby expected at any moment, she was spending more time talking to her Father and reading His Word.

Footsteps sounded on the stairway, and a voice called to her.

"Mama! Make Joe stop teasing me!" Eight-year-old Annie charged through the door ahead of her brothers. Joe was behind her, grinning broadly. Maria glanced at him, then back at Annie's distressed face.

"Now what?"

"Mama, he says we have enough girls in this family and our new baby will be another boy! He says I can go and stay with Rosie if I want a girl to play with."

Maria hugged her daughter. "Joe doesn't have anything to say about the new baby. If God wants to send us a girl, He will do it. Joe, since you have nothing better to do than to torment your sister, you can carry the trash down for me."

NEAR THE END OF JANUARY, MARY JOINED THE family on 21st Avenue. Annie was delighted with a baby sister, and the boys were pleased, too. Maria kept busy with her growing family, and she continued to pray for each one of them daily by name.

Very shortly after the baby arrived, 10-year-old Joe had reason to be thankful that his name was on the list.

The Melrose theater was crowded with boys and girls on a Saturday afternoon. Everyone waited to see the latest Western, and Joe was among them. Seated in the balcony, he watched wide-eyed as the cowboy in the white hat captured the outlaw and peace returned to the town. A newsreel and cartoons were next, then the main feature was repeated. Joe decided to stay and see it again.

At dinner time, Maria questioned Dominic.

"Where is Joe?"

"He went to the movies, Mama."

"That was a long time ago. Where is he now? Go see if you can find him. Dinner is ready."

Dominic ran down to the theater, but Joe was nowhere in sight.

"He must have gone home with one of his friends," Dominic reported. "I didn't see him there."

It grew dark early in winter, and Maria was concerned when the boy didn't appear by bedtime. When the family had gone to bed, Maria sat down in her rocker and prayed for Joe.

He didn't get in with bad company she was sure, but he did do things his mother considered daring.

IN THE THEATER BALCONY, JOE OPENED HIS EYES and sat up. He must have dozed off. Dimly he could see the outline of rows of seats around him, but there didn't seem to be anyone in them, and there was nothing shining on the screen in front of him. Where was everyone?

Quickly Joe made his way downstairs to the front lobby. No lights there, either, except one small bulb over the popcorn and candy counter. He was able to make out by that faint light that the clock said 2 o'clock. A glance at the outside street assured Joe that it wasn't two in the afternoon.

His heart sank. What was Mama going to say? Maybe she was already in bed and asleep. Even as he ran toward the big front door, this didn't seem like a great possibility to him. The worst was yet to come. The door was locked. *All* the exit doors downstairs were chained and padlocked. What would he do now?

Then Joe remembered seeing a ladder on the outside of the theater building. Perhaps the door to the fire escape wasn't chained! Back up the stairs he clambered. The heavy metal door was unlocked. As he climbed out onto the grilled floor of the fire escape, the cold night wind whipped through his coat. Joe realized that the end of the ladder didn't reach the ground.

There was no choice, however. The door into the balcony had slammed shut behind him. He would have to risk a broken bone and jump from the bottom rung. That wasn't necessary. Joe took three or four steps down, and the ladder slid to the pavement with a horrible screech and clatter. Surely everyone in Melrose Park had heard the racket. With his heart thudding furiously, the little boy took off running toward home. What Mama might say no longer concerned him. He only wanted to see her!

Maria heard him pounding up the stairs and thanked the Lord for bringing him home safely. Joe threw his arms around her and sobbed out his fright. "But I knew you were praying for me," he concluded. "I knew you wouldn't go to bed and forget about me."

"Never," Maria told him, "never will I do that."

IN ADDITION TO CHURCH SERVICES IN THE NEW mission each week and calling house to house in many neighborhoods, Maria felt that there was more she could be doing for the Lord. At church she voiced a suggestion.

"I feel that the Lord is leading me to witness in public," she said. "Some of us should go out on Saturday evening to testify and sing on the street corner downtown. There the people who are shopping will hear us."

"The Salvation Army is already down there every week," someone told her. "They have played instruments and preached on the corner for years."

"We can join them. They will be glad to have more singers. Maybe they need people who will testify in Italian. We can do that."

Several members agreed to go the following Saturday, and Maria and the older children were among those who joined the Army musicians. A large crowd gathered to listen, not all of them sympathetic to the message. This didn't deter Maria. When she realized that she was too small to be heard or seen over the heads of the crowd, she sent Joe to get a box for her to stand on. She spoke without hesitation about what great things the Lord had done for her. She assured them that He would do the same for them if they would place their faith in Christ Jesus.

On the outskirts of the group of listeners, two men were walking home from work. They stopped to see what was going on.

"Mr. Mannoia, isn't that your wife up there talking?"

Vincenzo was embarrassed. "Yes, I guess it is," he muttered. "Come on, I need to get home."

"You need to keep a closer watch on your wife," his friend suggested. "She is known all over town. Some people call her a troublemaker."

Vincenzo defended Maria. "She is a good wife. She never neglects her family or her home. I know she has turned against the church for this new belief, but it has made her a better person. I see the love of God in her."

Fortunately, Vincenzo didn't see the hatred of some of

the onlookers that was directed against the musicians and speakers. Tomatoes, rocks and potatoes were hurled at the group, along with curses and insults. If they thought such actions would deter the Protestant Christians, they soon found out differently. The meetings continued to be held on the corner.

Maria was philosophical about the situation.

"What goes around, comes around," she said to Rose. "I spent my youth throwing vegetables at the Salvation Army in Sicily. Now I'm getting some of my own back again. If this is the price for serving the Lord, it is not too great for me. I have joy in my heart."

One day as Maria went about her errands, she passed the welfare center where many were waiting to receive their rations. This, she thought, was an excellent opportunity to testify! These people were not going anywhere very soon. Reaching into her handbag, Maria drew out tracts and gospels. From one to another she moved, offering a tract and telling each person what the Lord Jesus Christ had done for her. She wasn't discouraged when some refused to look at the tracts or listen to her testimony.

The Holy Spirit would reach their hearts, she thought. She had only to be faithful to what God called her to do.

Having found this new mission field, Maria was faithful to return often. One day as she stood outside the building to speak about Christ, a police car arrived. There were four officers, two who spoke English and two who spoke Italian. They left the car and approached Maria.

"Ma'am, we must inform you that you are breaking the law holding a public service without a permit. We'll have to ask you to leave."

"It is against the law to stand on the street and visit with my neighbors?"

"No, Ma'am. But you aren't visiting. You are preaching and handing out religious material."

"I am telling them what God has done for me," Maria said. "If I give them something good to take home and read, that's no more than any friendly person would do for her neighbors. We are talking quietly."

The officer shook his head. "We are required to acquaint you with the law and ask you to leave. If you persist, you will be arrested."

"I am now acquainted with the law," Maria replied. "I can't promise that I won't be back. But wait —" She dug into her bag again and thrust a tract into the hand of each officer. "Here, you need to trust Jesus Christ as your Savior. This will tell you how to do that. Now I will leave and I will see you again later."

The befuddled officers watched in disbelief as this little woman smiled at them and turned toward her home. They shrugged helplessly and pushed the tracts into their pockets as they returned to their car.

"This won't be the last we see of her," one declared. "I

remember when she was in court sometime back. She doesn't fear God or man." He pondered that for a moment. "Well, maybe God but not the judge."

Not long after that occasion, the officer found this to be true. Maria was again going from one person to another in a group gathered outside the office. Some of them were receptive and listened carefully to what Maria said. Others were rebellious and tried to stop her. But Maria had only one goal in mind: to obey her Lord and to make sure that everyone in Melrose Park heard about His power to save.

Silence descended upon the crowd when the police car pulled up and the officers approached Maria.

"Mrs. Mannoia, ..."

Maria beamed at him. "Yes, I remember you. Did you read the tract I gave you? Did you learn the true way to salvation?"

The officer looked flustered, but he went on with his business.

"Mrs. Mannoia, we will speak of that later. Now I will have to ask you to accompany me to the station. You were issued a warning about gathering a crowd on a public street and preaching without a permit, so ..."

"Oh, but they didn't come because I asked them. They were already here, and I felt I should speak to them."

The crowd watched quietly, looking from Maria to the officer as they spoke. Very few of the people, especially those who lived in Maria's neighborhood, felt that the side of the law would triumph in the battle. The young man knew when he had been beaten.

"All right, Mrs. Mannoia. We'll let the judge settle this. I can't tell you what's right or wrong. I'm just doing what I'm told."

The judge sighed as he listened to the charge brought before the little lady with whom he was familiar. He knew that he was required by law to do so, but he dreaded asking her a leading question.

"Have you anything to say, Mrs. Mannoia?"

"Yes. Is America a place where we have freedom to speak what is on our hearts in public?"

"It is. But a group such as you addressed can become unruly if they disagree with the speaker. We would then have a disturbance of the peace situation."

"They need to have their peace disturbed," Maria declared. "They must think of their eternal salvation and getting ready for heaven. I was only telling them ..."

The judge leaned wearily on his elbows and regarded Maria sternly.

"Mrs. Mannoia, why don't you go into the woods and preach?"

"The trees do not listen. The animals don't understand. But Jesus told us to preach to every creature, not to trees. Should I obey God or man? I must do as my Father commands me. The Lord has been so good to me, and I praise Him for all He does. He has kept me in safety and given me love for ..."

"Yes, yes, Mrs. Mannoia. I heard your testimony the last time you were here. Now please, I beg of you, be good enough not to appear in my court again. You are dismissed."

Maria rejoiced as she walked toward home. She had been about her Father's business, and she was content to know that many had heard the Word this day. His Word would not return unto Him void.

As she crossed the railroad tracks, Maria paused to look at the little depot that sat on the corner. Not only did the residents of Melrose Park pass here regularly, but anyone on the train going through town could not miss seeing a sign beside the station.

"I believe the Lord pointed it out to me," Maria told Rose and the boys. "I will do it at once."

Very soon a billboard appeared beside the Melrose Park depot:

ARE YOU READY TO MEET JESUS?
HE IS COMING SOON.

CHAPTER EIGHT

THE HEART OF THE HOME

The Mannoia family walked home from church through the alley to 21st Street. The service had lasted a little longer than usual, and everyone was hungry. Jimmy kicked a stone from his path.

"At least Mama didn't give our dinner away today," he remarked, "I'm starved."

"I heard that," Maria called back to him. "There are many poor people who need dinner more than we do. You had a big breakfast this morning. You should thank the Lord."

"I do, Mama. I'm thankful for every meal. You're the best cook in town."

As Maria ladled out the spaghetti with the tangy sauce and meatballs she had prepared the night before, she looked puzzled.

"I know I made more meatballs than this. Where are they?"

Five children appeared to be thinking about something else, and no one looked at her.

"Well? Did they just dissolve over night? Speak up. Dominic? Joe?"

"How many are missing, Mama?"

"How many did you eat, Dominic?"

"I guess one on the way to the bathroom. And maybe one on the way back."

"He came back to bed chewing it, and it smelled so good I had to get one — or two," Joe admitted.

One by one each child confessed to stopping in the fragrant-smelling kitchen and scooping out a couple of meatballs.

"And you thought I wouldn't notice? After this I'll count the meatballs when they go on the stove and when they come off. Any missing, and someone around the table has a tanned hide. Now, who wants to go to the Olive Branch Mission this afternoon?"

Everyone did. There was great adventure involved in visiting skid row in Chicago. The workers, as well as the homeless men who came for a meal and a place to clean up, were always happy to see the Mannoia family arrive. The little lady with the radiant face would praise the Lord and testify about His goodness. They all sang and often played instruments. Hardened men of the streets cried as they listened to Maria tell them what God could do in their lives.

The hour trip on the elevated train each way was a tiring one, but to Maria it was a labor of love to her Lord.

"You'll never forget these people," she said to the children. "They are precious souls in the sight of God. When we minister to them, we minister to Jesus Himself the Bible tells us."

Mary had stayed close to Maria as they sang and testified. Now she had a question.

"Why don't the men go home, Mama?"

"Most of them don't have a home. They've left their families and haven't been able to find work or a place to live. That's why Olive Branch is here, to help them out when they have nowhere to go. At the same time, the workers can tell the men about Jesus and how He died for them. It is a privilege for us to come and give them hope."

While all the children enjoyed accompanying their mother to the mission and being part of the Saturday night street meetings, the boys were not always well treated at school. This was an Italian-Catholic community; and their attendance at a Protestant mission brought persecution from the other children. The priests at the church and the teachers looked the other way when Dominic, Joe and Jimmy were ridiculed and shoved off the sidewalks.

Around the kitchen table, the situation was discussed.

"I don't like being shoved around because someone doesn't like the church I attend," Joe said. "One fellow said the priest told them to do it. Do you think he did, Mama?"

Maria shook her head. "I don't know. But I do know that Satan is behind it, no matter who he works through. He doesn't want people to find out about Christ dying on the cross for their sins, so he puts it into their hearts to do all they can to discourage you."

"They don't discourage me," Dominic declared. "I ask them to come to the mission and sing with us. Some of them have come, too."

"Some of my friends think I should fight back," Jimmy said. "But I don't like to fight. I just don't pay any attention."

As the youngest boy, Jimmy had a busy life. One important job was to take the bread to Mr. Magnolio, the baker.

"The bread is ready to go, Jimmy," Maria said to him. Maria had been up before daylight, mixing the dough in the big silver dishpan. Now it rested on the bed next to the radiator, rising and ready to be formed into loaves. Jimmy took the bread in his wagon in the afternoon and left it to be baked in the big ovens at the bakery. On the way home the next day, it was picked up and brought back. He didn't mind the job. The bakery was always warm in the winter and always smelled good. Just knowing that Mama had saved some of the dough for fried bread and pizza hurried Jimmy's steps on these days.

Another job that Jimmy had was a paper delivery route. One evening when he was about 10 years old, he had an experience that stayed with him the rest of his life.

Darkness came early in the winter. He didn't want to admit it to his brothers, but Jimmy was fearful as he finished his route and left the lighted street. This evening as he ran from the sidewalk on the way toward their steps in the alley, he stopped suddenly in panic. There, next to the brick garbage bin, stood a man in a long white robe. He had a crown on his head and a lantern in his hand. Jimmy felt his fear removed as the man looked at him as if to say, "You don't have to be afraid. Just follow me."

That night as Jimmy and Mary sat with Mama as she read the Bible to them, he had a warm feeling of security. The radiator beside him hissed, and Mama made the people in the Bible come alive to them. His decision was made. Jimmy would follow the Lord and the future would be all right. Never again would he fear the darkness of the alley as he returned home.

Saturday night was special to the younger children. Together with Maria, they would trudge through the alley, carrying their cleaning supplies, and ready the mission for the Sunday services. As they swept, dusted and polished, they sang together and visited happily.

"It makes Sunday better to know that we helped clean up the church, Mama. It smells and looks so good."

"I'd rather be a doorkeeper in the house of the Lord than to dwell in the palace of the king — or the tents of the wicked," Maria told them. "Some people think we should hire someone to clean the church, but even Jesus was a servant to His disciples. We shouldn't do less than He did. Remember that he who wants to be first must be a servant of all."

Maria did more than quote that admonition; she lived it.

There was no task too menial, no person too poor for her loving attention.

Melrose Park wasn't the only area that was the recipient of Maria's fervor. Many days she would travel to Chicago to evangelize and hand out tracts. Her efforts were not always met with joy and acceptance. The fashionable dress boutiques in the upper-class shopping districts were familiar with Maria Mannoia. Through her they were able to obtain the one-of-a-kind designs for women's clothing that were usually available only from Paris or Italy.

"Can you believe that plain little woman can turn out fashions like this with only a picture to look at?" Helene Le Fevre handled the garments that Maria had just brought in with reverence. They were the latest style and fabric and would bring a small fortune to Helene's Shoppe. Many Chicago women waited for Maria's work to appear.

"I don't believe she knows what an exquisite couturier she is," Helene continued. "I'm certainly not going to tell her."

"I'm sure she doesn't," Francine remarked. "Look what she's doing now."

The women walked to the window and watched as Maria spoke to the passers-by and handed each of them a leaflet.

"What is she doing? Is she advertising?"

"You could say that, Helene. But she's not advertising designer clothes. She's handing out gospel tracts and telling people to get right with the Lord."

Helene's face flushed red. "In front of *my* shop? Whatever will people think? What can I do about it?"

"They'll think she's an odd little lady. I wouldn't do anything about it. She brings in more people than she turns away," Francine laughed. "None of our clients will ever associate her tracts with *you*, Helene."

Had Maria been aware of the conversation inside the elegant shop, she would not have cared. Her heart was directed toward one goal in life: that everyone with whom she came in contact would know her Lord and the power of His resurrection. Ridicule didn't faze her. If her God was pleased with her efforts, nothing else mattered.

Thus it was that Maria and the children took full advantage of the World's Fair held in Chicago in 1933.

"I feel the Lord has put on my heart to attend the fair," she announced to the ladies in the church.

"We will all attend the fair one or two times while it is so close, Maria. What do you mean 'the Lord has put it on your heart'?"

"I will not just 'attend' one or two times. I'm not interested in looking around at the displays. I want to reach the people of every nation for the Lord."

The ladies looked at her blankly. "That's a pretty big order, Maria. How will you get the attention of the people who come to see the sights?"

"Yes, and how will you talk to them? They won't all be

Italian, you know. Even your English isn't perfect."

Maria waved away their objections. "That doesn't matter. The Lord will interpret for me. If He is with me, I won't worry about how they hear."

There was no problem with "getting their attention." Each morning Maria and the younger children would board the street car in Melrose Park and travel to the city. A transfer to the elevated train would take them to the entrance of the fair grounds. Accompanying them was a large sign attached to a two-part pole. "Prepare To Meet Thy God, O Nation" (Amos 4:12).

The banner couldn't be ignored as the throngs entered and left the big fair area. Truly people of all nations passed that way. Curious glances were sent in the direction of the little group gathered there. The smiling little woman and the children handed out tracts to all who would take them.

Some visitors mocked them and laughed at what they considered foolishness; others would bless them with a handshake. The Christians were glad to see the family and commended Maria as they passed by.

"Mama, look there!" Mary was excited. "Someone threw away one of the tracts, and that man picked it up. He's reading it!"

"I'm not surprised. The Lord said that His Word would not return to Him void, but accomplish that whereunto He sent it. We will never know how many people will be led to think about meeting God and take His message home to their families."

An elderly woman approached Maria and grasped her hand. The lady wept as she looked at the sign and the little group around it.

"God bless you for being here," she said to Maria. "This is the most important display at the World's Fair. I would like to have you come eat lunch with me. I am so happy to find Christians witnessing for the Lord in this place!"

Friends were made during those trips to the World's Fair. One gentleman from Holland was so taken with the family that he made several trips to their home in Melrose Park and sat on the porch to visit. Vincenzo was fascinated, but bewildered by him.

"Who is this 'Yimmy' he talks to? I can't understand half of what he says. He's a friendly man, though. Just needs to learn to speak Italian."

"Papa would be better off if some of the men who speak Italian didn't come around here," Dominic said to his mother. "They are out there again right now."

Maria nodded, and Dominic saw a determined look on her face as she heard the basement door open and close.

"I didn't mean that you should say anything, Mama. I'm sure everything will be all right."

"Never mind, Dominic. I will do as the Lord leads me. I think we've seen enough of those men."

As she continued preparation for dinner, Maria prayed

about the matter that plagued her. It had been nearly 20 years since they had left Sicily to make a home in America. The move had been prompted by fear of the Mafia. Now, as she reflected back over those years, she recalled that it hadn't been long until the Mafia, with their leader Al Capone, had arrived here also. They had been prominent in "Little Italy" in Chicago when the family moved to Melrose Park. Very soon the Mafia sought out their countrymen in that area.

Maria remembered the first visit to their home.

"Mama, there's some strange men in the yard talking to Papa. Who are they?"

Maria went to the window. She had not seen the men before, but she knew at once that they were not Vincenzo's co-workers. They were dressed in business suits and had an air of importance about them, even viewed from that distance.

When he came into the house after the men left, Vincenzo was silent. Maria could tell that he was shaken and upset. If it was so bad that he couldn't even shout about it, things must be terrible indeed. She waited for him to speak.

"They're here."

Maria didn't have to ask who "they" were. She knew at once.

"What did they say?"

"Very nice, they were. Very calm. They know we are new here, and because we are *'compadres,'* they want to be sure we are cared for. Since we don't know the language or understand the laws and justice in this new land, they will make sure that no one takes advantage of us."

Vincenzo's voice was deceptively quiet. "These men are young. They don't know what happened in Sicily 20 years ago. No one has told them that one of their Mafioso murdered my brother. They don't know how I hate them for what they've done. I didn't tell them I'd rather die than give them a percentage of my wages for their 'protection.' Men like that have no business living on this earth."

"What will you do?"

"Do? I have no choice. We heard this week that the fruit stand owner near the factory had acid thrown on him because he refused to pay. He is injured and his business is gone. How can I risk that for myself and my family?"

From that time on, the men would return regularly and speak briefly to Vincenzo. He would go into the basement, return with money which was handed to them. The men would smile pleasantly and leave.

Now, as Maria prayed about the situation, she felt that she must take action. She would go straight to the top and put a stop to this extortion once and for all.

Waukegan, the headquarters of "the capo," was a long streetcar and train ride from Melrose Park, but Maria was not deterred. She marched into the office and asked for an audience with the head of their organization. Perhaps because of the unusual sight of a determined little lady demanding the impossible, she was ushered into the inner sanctum and stood face to face with the leader of the Mafia, Al Capone.

The man who arose from behind the desk was not large or imposing. Had it not been for other sharp-eyed men standing about the office, this would have looked like any other business establishment. Maria knew it was not, and she prayed as she studied this one who seemed to be above and beyond the touch of the law.

"Yes, madam. How can I help you?"

Maria realized that she must speak quickly and clearly.

"My name is Maria Mannoia. My family and I live in Melrose Park. We came here from Misilmeri, Sicily, as did you yourself."

Capone's face darkened, but he continued to smile.

"This is true. But you have not come to say *'Buon giorno'* to a countryman, I assume."

"I have not. I am here to tell you that I know who you are, where you have come from, and what you do. I know every one of you, and if you don't stop bothering my husband, I'm going to report you to the police."

The two continued to study each other silently for several moments. Finally the man spoke.

"You have my word, Mrs. Mannoia. Now, good day to you."

Maria was escorted to the door, and as it closed softly behind her, a smile spread over her face. The Lord had been on her side again! Her cause had been right, and He had not forsaken her. Praise His name!

CHAPTER NINE

THE PRIEST IS NOT GOD

"MAMA, MAMA! COME QUICK!"

Maria turned from her stove as her little dark-haired girl rushed to the kitchen.

"Yes, Mary. What is it?"

"The parade. It's coming, and the statue is almost here. Hurry, Mama."

Mary tugged at her mother's apron, and Maria untied it. She would go with the child, though this annual event was one of the saddest occasions of the year for her. The Catholic church was holding a feast in honor of Mary, the mother of Christ.

Mother and daughter watched as the statue with the child came close to where they stood. The mother Mary was dressed in silk, her hair curled and her face made up. Gold rings adorned her fingers, and an ornate crown was on her head.

Men carried the heavy figure on a slab through the streets of the village on this day, confident that the people who adored the Holy Mother would toss coins on the statue. They stopped at houses along the street so that people could place money at her feet.

Mary stared wide-eyed at the marching bands, the paraders walking without shoes as a sacrifice, and the police with revolvers, protecting the money that was growing in amount as they watched.

"Look at all the gold jewelry she has on, Mama, and the crown. Aren't they beautiful?"

"She doesn't know anything about them, daughter. She can't use any of those things, or hear the singing, or see the 'Children of Mary' who follow her." Quiet tears rolled down Maria's face, and Mary pulled at her mother's skirt.

"Why are you crying, Mama?"

"All these souls that Jesus came to save! All these people love Mary more than Jesus, Who gave His very life for the world."

The main part of the parade passed by their gate, and Maria returned to the house, cautioning Mary not to leave the yard. After years of observing this celebration, Maria knew that the parade didn't end the day's festivities.

When all the village streets had been covered, the statue was again placed in front of the church where she could observe the party that went on into the night. A carnival atmosphere surrounded the area complete with fireworks and games. The aroma of frying sausages mingled with beer and wine as people ate and drank, sang and danced, and believed that they were honoring the Holy Mother by their celebration. In truth, Maria reflected, they were honoring Satan, the father of lies. Maria's heart was broken for the people of Melrose Park.

The feast of Mary wasn't the only "abomination" in Melrose Park over which Maria agonized and prayed. Another source of grief to her was a mountain which had been erected by the priests to represent Mount Calvary. At the top of the hill was a statue of Jesus, crucified. His mother Mary, Mary Magdalene and John were placed around the cross. Thirty-three steps led to the top.

From all around the area people came to worship there. They climbed the stairs on their knees, praying at each step. At the statue a feast was held like the one in the village.

"If they only knew how God will regard their work at the judgment," Maria lamented. "What can we do to turn hearts of the people in this village to the Lord?"

The ladies who attended the evening Bible studies talked it over.

"They need to hear the Word."

"They have to be warned of the punishment to come if they don't repent."

"They should know God loves them and wants to give them peace and salvation."

"We have tried. Whatever the Lord has told us to do, we have done. But the devil is battling everything we try. The sign is gone from the station."

Maria nodded. "I know. It was the perfect place for it, because everyone who came through Melrose Park saw it. They can't say at judgment that no one ever told them."

As Maria continued to pray about the matter, it seemed to her that she could not ignore the fact that what God had told her to do had been destroyed.

"I am going to put up another sign. This time it will be in the center of town," she announced at the dinner table.

"They'll take it down again, Mama," Dominic said skeptically. "More village people will see it and dislike it in town than at the station."

"That's what I intend. But I have a plan. This time I'll visit the president of Melrose Park. Maybe with permission, it will stay there."

Mr. Imburgio tapped his desktop thoughtfully and regarded the small lady in front of him. She was a force to be reckoned with, he knew. As president of the village he did his best to be diplomatic and to stay as far away as possible from any squabbles among the citizens. In particular, he dreaded the public disagreements between the churches. He had already had an uncomfortable conversation with Father Leo, who blamed this woman for every upheaval in the church since the Spanish Inquisition. He had been forced to try to explain why permission had been granted to allow a Protestant mission to be moved five blocks from his church without Father Leo's knowledge or consent.

Now Mrs. Mannoia was requesting permission to erect a sign on the busiest corner of town proclaiming the imminent return of the Lord. Mr. Imburgio found himself half-way wishing that the event might take place before he had to make a decision. It was not to happen, however, and being reasonably certain that the sign would not stay there for long, the president conceded.

"You may have permission, Mrs. Mannoia. But understand, there is no guarantee that it will remain there. The village takes no responsibility for protecting the sign or punishing its defacers."

Maria nodded. "That's all right. God takes responsibility for His own Word. Thank you for your help."

The sign painter listened to her request and stood with his pencil poised above the order form.

"Didn't I just do one of these for you a few weeks ago?"

"Yes, but it was torn down. You may not want to do another one, but I'm not going to give up. The Lord wants the people in Melrose Park to be ready to meet Him."

"All right," the printer shrugged. "It's your $3. It'll be ready by Friday."

Joe came in from school the following week with the news. "The sign's gone, Mama."

"I'll go back to the printer in the morning. We were right the first time. It belongs at the train station where everyone who travels by can see it."

When the new sign had been in place for three weeks,

Maria felt sure it would remain there. It did not satisfy her desire for a visible testimony and warning to those who didn't visit the Northwestern train depot, however. She felt the need for something that would speak to all the people who went about their affairs in Melrose Park.

In the spring, as Maria walked back and forth on her daily errands, she began to notice placards announcing the coming municipal elections. President Imburgio's term was ended, and a new man would take office. A plan began to form in Maria's mind, and she approached the church members with it.

"It will be well for us to choose the candidate we want to support," she told them. "We need a president who will be sympathetic to our church and not fight what we are trying to do."

"You're asking for a lot, Maria. Both of the candidates are strong Catholics. They'll receive much pressure from the church. I don't know why President Imburgio allowed you to put up that sign, but the new man may not be as friendly."

"I don't want another sign. The Lord has revealed to me that we should put a Bible in the public library!"

Mrs. del Sarto gasped. "A Bible! The priest would never allow it!"

"The priest is not in charge of the public library. The president and the trustees are the ones to give permission. Besides, the priest is not God. He doesn't have the final word on anything. The Lord is in charge."

"How do you plan to convince the trustees to allow this?"

"I have thought much about it. I will talk to the trustees and tell them that we in our church will give them our votes if they will let us put a Bible in the library."

After some discussion, the plan was approved, and Maria approached the men with her request. Perhaps the novelty of the suggestion intrigued the board, or perhaps they recognized the authority with which this little woman worked. They promised that it would be done.

A WEEK AFTER THE ELECTIONS, MRS. CALUCCI, the town librarian, was surprised and a bit overwhelmed by finding herself face to face with the new president of Melrose Park. He carried a leather-bound book under his arm which he handed to Mrs. Calucci.

"I've been requested to present this to the library." He cleared his throat nervously. "It's a gift from one of the citizens of the village."

The librarian looked at the book in disbelief.

"A Bible?" She flipped open the cover to the title page. "A *Protestant* Bible?"

"Yes, ma'am. That's what Mrs. Mannoia asked for."

"That woman must have a lot of influence with the board," Mrs. Calucci remarked to her assistant after the president left. "I wonder who she is?"

They were not left to wonder long. After a few days Maria entered the library and approached the desk.

"Has the Bible arrived?"

Mrs. Calucci looked at her carefully. This woman in the plain blue dress with the white collar, and hair pulled back from her face in a bun, didn't look like the influential citizen she had pictured.

"You are Mrs. Mannoia?"

Maria nodded.

"It is here." The librarian turned to a shelf behind the desk and removed the Bible. Maria held it in her hands, and tears rolled silently down her cheeks.

"Praise the Lord for His Holy Word. Now everyone can read it. Thank you. Thank you."

For several minutes after Maria had left, Mrs. Calucci stood holding the Bible and gazing at the door.

"That was Mrs. Mannoia," she said to her assistant as she replaced the book on the shelf. "I believe that woman walks with God."

Maria had not yet finished her task. Her next stop was the newspaper office. The townspeople didn't miss the notice in the paper that evening.

There is now a Bible in the Melrose Park Public Library. Go and see the greatest book in the world. It will bring light into your darkness.

THE VILLAGE OF ELMWOOD PARK LAY EAST OF Melrose Park on the outskirts of Chicago. Word came that the evangelist Nathan Beskin would be preaching there. Many Italian families lived in the town, and the Lord laid it on Maria's heart to work there. As she had been doing in Melrose Park, she began to call from house to house to witness for her Lord.

"Buono. My name is Maria Mannoia and I've come to give you some good news."

The woman at the door smiled and opened the screen.

"Come in. Come in. Good news is welcome here. We haven't heard much lately. My name is Lucia."

She looked closely at Maria.

"Have I seen you at church, Mrs. Mannoia? Not that I've been able to go lately, what with an invalid husband to care for and an elderly mother."

Maria was ushered into a cheerful room where a hospital bed sat in front of the window. A thin man with wispy hair welcomed her with a handshake.

"What is this good news you have?"

As Maria gazed around the room, she breathed a prayer for the right thing to say to these people. Surely the Lord had led her here.

"Jesus heals the brokenhearted."

Maria was startled. She had intended to quote a verse of Scripture. God must have put those words in her mouth. She hadn't thought of them beforehand.

Tears came into Lucia's eyes.

"Can this be true?"

Maria nodded. "It is true."

"Did you hear that, Lorenzo? An angel has come to tell us that Jesus heals the brokenhearted. How does this happen, Mrs. Mannoia? Does it really include us? What do we need to do?"

Carefully Maria laid out the plan of salvation for them. Then she shared her story of God's providence and goodness to her.

"We are brokenhearted because our son has left, and we haven't been able to see how we could manage alone. We want to accept this gift you speak of."

Together they prayed, and the presence of the Lord filled the room. When Maria rose to leave, Lucia took her to the door. "You will return, won't you? You'll come back and tell us more about this wonderful Lord?"

Maria assured her that she would.

"I'll tell the neighbors. They have hard times, too. Oh, how happy they'll be!"

All the way home on the streetcar, Maria rejoiced over the two new souls born into the kingdom.

"What if I hadn't gone there?" she wondered. "What if the Lord had not prepared their hearts?"

On Sunday, Maria reported to the church her experience in Elmwood Park.

"The Lord said to go into all the world and preach the gospel, and 'Lo, I am with you always.' He was with me this week, and I feel that we should have a group to go to that village. They have no one to tell them what the Lord can do, and they are hungry for the Word. We must share with them all that the Lord has given to us."

Maria was persuasive, and in the weeks that followed, five more families were brought into the circle. Once each week Brother Simon took the group to Elmwood Park for prayer and Bible study in the homes. A Sunday school was started in the basement of the small church, and 50 children were nurtured by the new Christians.

Her friends didn't always understand Maria's zeal.

"You have so much to do here, how do you have time to go to other neighborhoods and call on the people? Isn't Melrose Park a big enough job for you?"

"The Lord wants me to speak," Maria replied, "so I seek to help them. Brother Shelhammer said if we see a house burning in the neighborhood, don't we go immediately to help them? And so when we see a soul in danger of hell, should we not help them? I must do as the Lord directs. He will give the strength and the time for His work."

Watching Maria's life, few had reason to disagree with her.

CHAPTER TEN

"GO ... UNTO JUDEA"

THE SOUND OF MUSIC FLOATED FROM THE kitchen to the living room where Mary and Jimmy sat in front of the radio listening to "Little Orphan Annie."

"Precious Lord, take my hand
Lead me on, let me stand
I am tired, I am weak
I am woe ..."

"Mama. It's 'I am *worn,'* not woe," Mary called to her.

The music stopped. "Never mind. My precious Lord knows what I'm saying. Sometimes I am woe, too. As soon as the program ends, get ready for dinner. Papa will be here soon."

Before long Papa's voice was heard calling from the stairway. "Jimmy! Come and help me with my boots!"

The evening ritual began. Jimmy pulled and tugged on the snow and ice encrusted boots while Papa hung on to his heavy socks and complained about the time it took to remove them.

"Put those boots on the newspaper, Jimmy. I don't want to mop the whole floor again."

Mama shook her head at her husband. "I left the broom down there so you could sweep off your pant legs and boots. You didn't need to tramp it upstairs."

"It's cold out there." He removed his coat and put on an old sweater that hung on a hook by the door. "It's cold in here, too. What's the matter with the furnace?"

Papa padded in stocking feet to the living room and checked the thermostat on the wall.

"It isn't even 70 degrees in here!" he roared. "Who's been pushing the thermostat down?" Quickly he pushed it to 85 degrees, where it remained until he retired for the night.

"It's a good thing your father goes to bed early," Maria remarked as she pushed the thermostat down. "Joe, did you add water to the boiler when you tended the furnace? I don't want Papa waving the poker at me the next time he goes down there. And the language he uses! He thinks *he* never forgets to fill the boiler. I'm the one who gets the blame."

"You should stay up here with your kitchen and sewing machine, Mama. Let Papa worry about his boiler and his winepress."

WHEN SCHOOL WAS OUT IN THE SPRING, MARIA and the children looked forward to the brightest days of their summer — two weeks of camp meetings. Located in Glen Ellyn, and later in Downer's Grove, IL, the event was similar to those held in each state around the country.

The campground smelled wonderful. Soft pine needles lay on the ground. And little puffs of dust arose from the roads that ran around the perimeter of the camping area. Large trees towered overhead, and a breeze seemed to banish the July heat that hung over the countryside. Home seemed a long way off, although only a few small villages stood between Downer's Grove and Melrose Park.

On the morning camp began, Mr. Scanio's grocery truck deposited the family and their belongings at the site Maria had chosen — not too far from the large tabernacle that was at that moment being furnished with platform, benches and fresh sawdust.

Maria directed the setting up of camp.

"Dominic and Joe, you go over and get the tent and put it right here in the shade. You girls can fill the ticks with straw. Carry them back here on your shoulders; don't drag them in the dust. Jimmy, set up the army cots and put a nail in the tree for the towel."

An apple crate under the mirror held the wash basin, soap and combs. Maria took charge of stretching a rope for a clothesline, and very soon home was ready for the next two weeks.

"It was a wonderful meeting," Maria reported to Rose when they returned home. "I attended every service and praised the Lord for His goodness." She continued to scrub the clothes in the big tub. "I'm afraid some of the women who claim to be saved and sanctified aren't living up to all the light they have. I spoke to one lady who painted herself up like the world."

"The Bible says you shouldn't judge the other people, Mama."

"That's what the superintendent said, too."

"The superintendent talked to you about it?"

Maria nodded. "The lady complained about me. But I'm used to that. I told him that 1 Corinthians 2:15 says 'The spiritual man judges all things.' I do what the Bible tells me to do. Maybe the lady will think about it before she paints herself up again."

"You're not going to win any popularity contest, Mama."

"The Bible doesn't say we have to do that."

Maria went on about her work, secure in the belief that she was following the Lord.

AS THE WEEKS WENT BY, AND THE ITALIAN mission in Melrose Park continued to grow, Maria's influence widened to other communities around the Chicago area. The success of the mission did not escape the attention of Brother Howard, the Evanston church member who had moved the church building to its present location.

"Our church is prosperous and growing here in Evanston," he said to his wife one evening. "But it concerns me that we aren't reaching the Italian families in this area. When I see what has happened in Melrose Park and Elmwood Park, I feel that we are failing to reach out past our own Jerusalem."

"There is no one in our church who can minister to the Italians, even if we brought them in. No one speaks their language well enough."

"I know someone who does," Brother Howard replied. "Mrs. Mannoia has started several Bible study groups in 'Little Italy' in Melrose Park."

"That's quite a distance from here, John. She may not have transportation for a trip like that."

"I think we can work that out. I'll talk to her."

MARIA WIPED HER HANDS ON HER APRON AND greeted her visitor.

"Have a seat, Brother Howard. Let me move the sewing out of your way. Now, what brings you to Melrose Park?"

Brother Howard looked around the room at the fabric and the garments that were being worked on. Bolts of material lay on the table and an unfinished dress was draped over the sewing machine.

"I'm afraid I've come at a busy hour, Sister Mannoia. Do you have time to talk for a few minutes?"

"Oh, my, yes. I always have time for my friends. Have you heard how the Lord is blessing our church?"

"Indeed I have. That's one of the reasons I'm here. I want to ask you to 'come over to Macedonia' and help us. Evanston has a number of Italian families that aren't being reached for the Lord. Would you be interested in coming to call on them?"

"Wherever the Lord opens the way for me to testify for Him, I will go," Maria declared. "Tell me where these people live, and I will bring the Lord to them."

"I'll take you there the first time, and thereafter I'll pay your transportation. Perhaps you could begin Bible studies in the homes and pray with them. We feel that they need someone who understands them and speaks their language."

MRS. BRIDGMAN STOOD AT HER FRONT WINDOW and parted the curtains slightly. A look of distaste crossed her countenance.

"There she is again," she muttered.

Mr. Bridgman lowered his paper.

"Who?"

"That horrible woman who has been walking around the neighborhood lately."

"Do you know her?"

"Of course not!"

"Then how do you know she's horrible?"

"Oh, Harry. For goodness' sake. You just have to *look* at her to know. She doesn't look like us."

Mr. Bridgman rose from his chair and peered over his wife's shoulder.

"She looks all right to me. Does a lady have to wear a fur coat in order to walk down Willowbrook Drive?"

Mrs. Bridgman glared at her husband.

"A *lady* doesn't walk the streets."

"Maybe she works around here."

"No, she doesn't. I've asked. She calls on people and ... (here Mrs. Bridgman shuddered) preaches to them!"

Mr. Bridgman suppressed a smile.

"Some folks on this street could use it. Has she called here?"

"Absolutely not!" Mrs. Bridgman dropped the curtain and turned from the window. "She'd better not, either. I'll give her a piece of my mind!"

I'm sure you will, Mr. Bridgman thought, *whether you can spare it or not.*

Maria had no intention of stopping there, since this was not an Italian family to which she had been introduced. Since Brother Howard had brought her to Evanston some weeks before, she had been busy ministering to those she'd met. It was not in Maria's nature, however, to pass by a stranger without speaking to her. "Speaking," to Maria, meant telling the stranger about her Lord.

Thus it was that Maria was proceeding up this same street one day as Mrs. Bridgman clipped roses for her ladies tea. The woman did not see her approach.

"Buon giorno."

Mrs. Bridgman whirled around to find Maria standing beside her.

"Hasn't God given us a beautiful day?"

Weeks of aggravation burst out as the woman stared at Maria.

"Who are you, anyway? What are you doing here?"

"I'm Maria Mannoia, and I'm working for my Lord. He has told me to take the gospel to all people, and I'm doing it. Have you found the Lord as your Savior?"

Mrs. Bridgman stepped back, and her face flushed.

"We do not need the gospel preached to us on this street or in this town! Let me warn you, Mrs. Mannoia, if I see you here again, I'll, I'll throw you in the lake!"

Furiously she turned and marched back to the house, oblivious to the fact that she carried only two roses, scarcely enough to provide a decent centerpiece for her table.

That evening Maria reported the events of her day to the family.

"Weren't you scared, Mama?" Mary looked troubled.

Maria smiled. "No. The Lord is my guardian, and I don't fear threats like that. She wasn't big enough to throw me very far."

She turned back to the stove and slowly stirred the sauce that bubbled in the pot. Her smile broadened.

"She was wearing one of the dresses I made."

MARIA WAS PUZZLED. SHE STOOD IN FRONT OF the large factory in Chicago several weeks later and watched the employees enter for the day's work.

"Why did you send me here, Lord? I don't need the job.

Is there someone here that I'm supposed to minister to?"

Earlier in the week, Maria had felt that the Lord wished to have her apply for employment at this company.

"Why would you go there, Maria? That is a Jewish business. Is there someone in that company that you know?"

Mrs. Luigi was curious. "It sounds like the Lord wants you in Judea now!"

Maria didn't know, but she applied for a job and was accepted. To her surprise, there were many Italian employees from different places. She lost no time in testifying to them. Each day she carried her Bible, and during the lunch hour it lay on the table where all could see it.

"I have many Jewish friends there," she reported to the ladies at the church. "They want me to talk to them."

"But they don't want to hear about Jesus, Maria. What did you tell them?"

"I tell them how the Lord brought me out of the Catholic church and opened my eyes to His precious will. We read the Bible together."

Maria recalled the day that she opened her Bible to Isaiah 53.

"Do you know of the prophet Isaiah?" she asked them.

Yes, they knew of him.

"But did you know that Isaiah told us about Jesus many centuries before He was born?"

Blank looks met that statement, and Maria nodded

happily. "Isaiah told us that Jesus carried our sorrows and died for our sins. Listen to what he said:

' ... because he poured out his life unto death, and was numbered with the transgressors. For he bore the sin of many, and made intercession for the transgressors' (Isaiah 53:12).

"Now if your own prophet tells you what Jesus did for you, shouldn't you love Him with your whole heart?"

For many days Maria continued to talk with her Jewish friends and point them toward the true light. Many believed and listened carefully to her testimony. One day following the lunch hour, the boss approached her with tears in her eyes.

"Maria, pray for me," she said.

"Oh, how my heart rejoiced," Maria told her friends at the church. "All of those people have heard the Word, and it will not return to Him void. This was the reason I was sent to work at the factory where they are all Jewish. I believe I will meet many of them in heaven."

At home and abroad, Maria continued to spread the good news of God's love to strangers and neighbors alike. As she neared her 60th birthday, the world prepared for another war.

CHAPTER ELEVEN

WAR AT HOME AND ABROAD

IN THE LATE 1930S IT WAS OBVIOUS THAT THE world was again headed for war. Factories began gearing up to produce ammunition, aircraft and other implements of warfare. In 1938, President Roosevelt proposed appropriations for military expansion to keep the country defensively strong. A resolution in the House of Representatives called for a national referendum to decide a declaration of war.

"Who in his right mind would vote for war?" Maria wondered. "I don't know any parents who would send their boys across the seas to fight."

That proposal was shelved, but the following year Roosevelt asked Congress for a $535 million defense appropriation. Clearly preparations were being made for U.S. involvement, although the president declared American neutrality in a public speech.

In 1940, Joe was the first to come home with the news that all men between the ages of 21 and 36 were required to register for military service.

"That includes me, Mama. I don't have a reason to be deferred like Dominic and Jimmy have. They are both in college and preparing for the ministry. Besides, Jimmy isn't old enough yet."

"Maybe you won't be called right away, Joe. Your job is important."

"Being a chef *is* important, but it isn't essential to the war effort. I'm going to enlist, Mama!"

Suddenly, after so many years with children running up the steps, Maria and Vincenzo found themselves without a child at home. Mary and Anne were also in school, and when Joe left for England, Maria's daily prayers for each one of them, in order, took on a greater urgency.

New sewing assignments came to Maria because of the war. Many a G.I. went into battle wearing a uniform that was hand-crafted at home by a master seamstress. As important as that was, to Maria it could not compare with the assignment given to her by the young man who worked with the youth in the church.

"I don't know what the mission would do without Brother Hensell," Maria said to Rose. "Have you been down in the basement to see the room he's fixed up for the young people?"

"Brother Hensell? The Sunday school superintendent? I

know he's done a lot of work in the church. I went in one day while he was varnishing the seats and floors. He's certainly made the church look like new. How does he happen to be so interested in our mission? He doesn't even live in Melrose Park, does he?"

"No, but he loves the Italians. He takes charge of the Christmas and Easter programs as well as the Y.P.M.S. (youth) group. The Lord will reward him for his work."

The patriotic fervor that swept the nation was soon evident in the Italian Mission. In the fall, Brother Hensell suggested that an American flag should be placed in the church.

"The flag represents the liberty we have to serve God," he told the members. "We have the freedom to preach in all places and to witness about Christ, and no one can impede us. We should honor our country's flag in our church."

It was decided that the new flag would be dedicated at the Christmas program. Before this event took place, Brother Hensell appeared at Maria's door with a large package.

"It will be wonderful to have an American flag in the church, Sister Mannoia, but I feel that we must not forget the flag of victory, the Christian flag." He placed the package on the table.

"I've brought the material for it. Would you have time to sew it up on your machine?"

"Of course I will," Maria replied. "I *make* time to work for my Lord. It won't take long at all." The flag took longer than

Maria anticipated. Rose stopped in one afternoon to find her mother sitting in her rocker with the flag in her lap. She was sewing the red cross on the white background by hand, and as she stitched, tears fell on the work.

"Mama? What are you doing? And why are you crying?"

"I couldn't sew the cross on the machine," Maria answered. "I have to put in one stitch at a time. It breaks my heart to think of the blood that Jesus shed on the cross for my sins. I've been thinking of His wonderful love that He had to go to Calvary for people who don't care anything about Him. Oh, if I could only do more to bring our neighbors to Christ!"

In spite of Maria's godly life and daily witness to the families who lived around her, there were still those who persecuted the faithful ones of the church. One of these individuals was a woman named Mrs. Fiori. She had lived near the Mannoia's home for many years, and she had never ceased to speak out against the Protestants. Perhaps because Maria was the most open and persistent in her witness for the Lord, Mrs. Fiori's war of attacks and profanity were most often directed toward her. In spite of the woman's hostility, Maria continued to speak to her and pray for her.

One day as Maria hung clothes in the yard, her friend Lucy Amati came to the fence to talk with her.

"Maria, you haven't seen Mrs. Fiori lately, have you?"

Maria took the clothespins from her mouth and shook her head.

"No, I haven't. It seems to me that the last time I saw her, she looked awfully thin. Do you think she is sick?"

Lucy nodded. "I know she is. She has tuberculosis. Her son tells me that she is in serious condition. She's been to many doctors, but they all told her that they weren't able to help her. They said that only God can help her now."

"Oh, my. The poor lady."

"Poor lady! After the way she bad-mouthed the church and the people in it, you sympathize with her? I say she's getting what she has coming."

"That is Satan working through her. He will use anyone who is willing to help him bring hardship to Christians. I'll pray for her especially this afternoon."

Later that week, Maria answered a knock at the door to find Mike Fiori, her neighbor's son, standing there.

"Mrs. Mannoia, Mama sent me over here to say that she wants to talk to you."

Quickly Maria removed her apron and threw a shawl around her shoulders. As she hurried through the alley, she prayed that the Lord would give her the right words to say to the sick woman. She must be near death, Maria thought, or she never would have called her long-time enemy to come to her home.

In the kitchen, Mr. Fiori and some of his friends were playing cards around the kitchen table. The game was interrupted while he took Maria into another room and told her of the condition his wife was in. Maria felt that the Lord was leading her to be bold and to ask largely.

Mrs. Fiori spoke weakly. There was no profanity or abuse now.

"Mrs. Mannoia, I am not long for this earth."

Maria wasted no time but came straight to the point of her visit.

"Mike brought the message that you wanted to talk to me. Let me ask you something, Mrs. Fiori. Do you believe that God can heal you if it is His will that you live longer?"

"Yes."

"Do you have faith in God that He can answer prayer?"

"Yes."

"If you believe and accept in your heart that God will hear your prayer, you will see His glory."

Together they prayed, and Maria called upon the Lord for help, forgiveness and healing. The hand that Maria held in her own relaxed, and Mrs. Fiori appeared contented.

"Don't forget that the Lord is on His throne and is in control of all our life. He is the same yesterday, today and tomorrow. Pray directly to Him, and He will hear you."

Back home in her kitchen, Maria praised God for His goodness and sang as she went about her work.

The next morning Mike appeared at the door again. "Mama rested well last night — the first in a long time. She said that what you have told her all these years is true. She says we are to come to church, if you'll have us."

One by one the Fiori family began to attend the mission. As the weeks went by, Mrs. Fiori healed completely, and she requested that the ladies have prayer meetings in her home.

"The Lord has glorified His Holy name!" Maria declared. "Praise the Lord!"

JOE FELICIA WAS IMPRESSED BY THE RETURN OF his sister from near death as a result of the prayers of those Protestant Italians at the mission near his home. Although he was obviously pleased that Angela was well, it had no visible effect upon his life or habits.

If asked, he probably would have said *his* life might be near its end if he chose to change his career at this point. Joe was a dealer in moonshine liquor and worked for Al Capone. Had this not been sufficient consideration, he enjoyed his evenings and nights of card games, gambling and pool. His lack of concern for his wife and four children didn't escape the notice of Maria, and one Saturday night she went to visit him.

"He's not here," his wife reported. "He's at the pool room. I don't know when he'll be home."

"Since you're alone, maybe you'd like to come to the prayer meeting," Maria suggested.

"Oh, I couldn't. If he came back and found me gone, there's no telling what he'd do."

"It breaks my heart to see that poor pitiful little woman,

without God or any comfort," Maria said to the ladies who gathered for prayer. "I should think her husband would be so grateful for what the Lord has done for his sister that he'd be anxious to come to church."

Maria was unable to sleep that night, thinking about the poor woman. She prayed that the Lord would have mercy on the family. In the morning at 7:30 she went and called at the house again.

"Will your husband come to church this morning?"

"I haven't asked him. He's still asleep because he didn't come home until 2 a.m."

"I will come back later and ask him myself," Maria said.

At 8:30 a.m. he was still in bed, so Maria made her way to the Fiori home.

"Mr. Fiori, would you call on your brother-in-law and tell him that your whole family will be attending church this morning? Maybe he will come with you if you invite him."

The Lord prepared everything. Joe attended church that morning and also in the weeks to follow. He was saved and left his former life behind him. The entire Felicia family became regular members of the mission and were used in God's work.

Only heaven will reveal how many souls were drawn to God because of Maria's faithfulness to the Holy Spirit.

IF ONLY ONE ADULT MEMBER OF A FAMILY BEcame a Christian and began attending the mission, it was usually the wife and mother. In many instances the father followed her lead, and due to her witness and prayers became a Christian also. Such was not the case with the Caliano family. Vincent, the husband, attended church regularly and often brought the children with him. In spite of his attempts to explain the gospel to her, his wife Sue could not bring herself to accept the Lord and leave the Catholic church. Maria befriended her, as she did all the neighborhood ladies, but was unable to persuade her to follow the lead of her husband and pray for salvation.

On a cold winter morning, Maria hurried along Lake Street on her way to the store. Suddenly, Sue Caliano rushed from her house, and Maria saw that she was crying.

"What's wrong, Sue?"

"Oh, Maria. It's Poli. She has such a high fever that I'm going to call the doctor. She is very sick."

"Come, Sue. Let's go back home and I will pray for her. I have faith that the Lord will heal her."

The 2-year-old girl was indeed ill. Her fever was so high that she was unable to breathe normally. Quickly Maria began to pray for the child as she bathed her with cool water. At once the fever began to subside, and Maria gave God the glory.

"The Lord has touched her by His grace, Sue. If you will serve Him, you will see more of His wonderful work in your life."

But Sue was not yet willing to submit to God's will. It took a threat to her own life to frighten her into believing that she needed to accept the Lord.

In February, Vincent reported to the church that his wife had fallen sick with a bad heart. One Saturday night when she found herself in distress, Sue committed her life to the Lord and asked forgiveness for her sins. When she had opened her heart and accepted the Lord's grace, she shouted with joy and praised God. The family that lived upstairs knocked on the door to inquire what was happening.

"I praise the Lord for His goodness," Maria said to her friends. "This proves that we must never give up praying for the lost. In God's time they will come to Him and be healed of their sins. Sue has been touched in body and soul. We must continue to be faithful in prayer."

ON JUNE 6, 1944, AMERICAN TROOPS LANDED on Normandy Beach in France. Joe Mannoia was among those who began a summer of unforgettable warfare. Maria wrote to her son faithfully and never ceased to pray for him. From Normandy to Saint Lo and on to the Rhone River, Joe's battalion pushed into Germany.

The enemy was using shells that exploded 50 feet above ground just like an umbrella. Joe, on top of a tank, was hit in the back and both legs. He was moved into a 10 foot bomb crater and left, with the promise that someone would come to get him.

As he lay in the crater, praying, Joe's mind went back over his years at home in Melrose Park. He felt Mama's latest letter in his pocket. Written in Italian, it was a source of great comfort to him. Even more reassuring was the fact that he knew that Mama was praying for him. He recalled the night that he had been locked in the movie theater at the age of 10. He remembered the trips he had made with the family to Olive Branch Mission on Sunday afternoons. He could see how Mama's face glowed when she was talking about God.

As the sun was going down, Joe prayed hard. Just then he heard his Mama praying, as though she were by his side. It was comforting to hear her voice. It was wonderful to have her presence beside him.

As Joe told the family later, "God continued to answer Mama's prayers. Because of the extent of my injuries, the doctor was going to amputate my leg. I pleaded with him not to cut it off, and the decision was made to try to save it. I knew Mama was praying for me."

To the delight of everyone, especially Jimmy, Joe appeared at Jimmy's graduation from Greenville College. Walking with crutches following his ordeal, Joe didn't hesitate to credit the prayers of his mother and the grace of God for his safe return home.

CHAPTER TWELVE

WAS IT WORTH IT ALL?

THE SUMMER SUN WAS SETTING AS MARIA rocked slowly on the porch of her home. Neighbors strolling by waved to her and called out, "Good evening, Maria." She smiled and waved, then her hands lay quietly in her lap again. It had been only recently that her hands had not been busy with some kind of work when she sat to rest.

It was now 1963, and she had lived many years in this home the Lord provided for her. She looked out over the plot that had been Papa's garden and held his prized hotbed. Papa had been gone now for ... how long? Thirteen years. Brother Bush was the pastor at the church then, and he had hurried over to be with her during Papa's last hours. Life had not always been easy with him, but Vincenzo had been a good man, and he loved his children.

Maria's thoughts turned to the children. Jimmy was the farthest away. He and his family had been in Brazil for a year now, but he kept in touch with his mama as did all the others. They wrote and called and visited regularly, and made sure that her every need was taken care of. She didn't need much. She had her home, her church and her friends. And she had her memories, almost 80 years worth of them.

Not all the memories were happy ones, she reflected, but then, whose were? Praise the Lord, He had never left her nor forsaken her.

As she rocked, Maria's mind went back to the many times she had suffered persecution for the sake of Christ. Her friends had offered advice and urged her to retaliate.

"At least defend yourself, Maria. There's no reason why you should stand there and let yourself be attacked."

"Vengeance belongs to the Lord. He will protect me from my enemies. If I do to them what they do to me, I'm no better than they are."

This conversation had taken place after the funeral for Joe Felicia's mother, Maria recalled.

Mrs. Felicia was a strong Catholic, well known and respected in the community. When she died, all the friends who were now members of the mission attended the funeral. Following the service, some of them went to the cemetery, but Maria and Rose turned to go home. Suddenly from the corner of the church, four women approached Maria and began to berate her.

"How do you dare show up in this church after what you have done to this community?"

"We know why you changed religions. You planned to

make money from the Protestants. You will do anything to make money. How else can you send all your children to school?"

Maria stood silent as they surrounded her with profanity and false accusations. When they saw that she would not respond, one of the women began to choke her. Still Maria did not resist. The priest who conducted the funeral stood by encouraging the women to attack her.

"I don't understand why you wouldn't at least take their hands from your neck, Mama," Rose said when they were finally able to leave. "You could have been killed."

"God was with me. He wouldn't allow them to harm me. My work here isn't done yet."

God had protected her, Maria thought. And He allowed things to come into the lives of the women that surely had caused them to consider their wickedness. One lady became gravely ill and spent the rest of her life in an iron lung. Another had an illness that caused her to lose the use of her feet and hands. The third died of stomach cancer.

Maria recalled these events with sadness. Had she done all she could do to befriend them and lead them to the Lord?

As she continued to rock and think back over the past years, Maria was reminded of one of the many confrontations she'd had with various members of the Melrose Park Police Department. She had certainly been no stranger to them, or to the judges before whom she stood.

"Maria, you should be careful about speaking up in the

court. One day the judge will put you in jail for contempt."

"I only speak when the Lord tells me I must. If I fear man, I can't serve the Lord."

The day stood out clearly in Maria's mind, and she smiled to herself as she remembered the circumstances. She really had taken a chance that time.

The 15th Avenue Free Methodist Church was having a revival, and all members of the Italian mission attended the service each evening.

Following church on this night, Maria and two friends were walking home, when suddenly from the back of the grocery store, the husband of one of the women emerged and began to beat and kick his wife. She screamed, and the police arrived. They immediately arrested the man and transported him and all the ladies to the police station to appear before the judge. Officer Passarella explained the circumstances.

"Suppose you tell me why you were beating your wife?" the judge said to the man.

"Because I don't want her going to a Protestant church," he replied. "She has no right to be there."

"If it is for that reason, you are to be condemned, because you could have killed her and committed a crime."

At this point, officer Passarella entered into the discussion.

"The husband is the head of the house and the owner of the wife!" he declared.

This has gone far enough, Maria thought. *He can't get*

away with that. She also stood and presented her opinion as she felt God would have her do.

"The husband is the head of the body, but not the soul; the soul is of God Whom it serves. The husband has no right to forbid his wife, for she has all the liberty to go to church where she wants to. Not even the law can stop her."

The astonished judge opened his mouth to speak, but officer Passarella was quick to move. He grabbed Maria by the arm. With one hand he opened the door, and with the other he threw her out of the room.

"Away with you! You are nothing but trouble here. You've put this village in ruins!"

He continued to shout as Maria calmly left the building and proceeded toward home, praising the Lord for what she considered a victory.

"Maybe you'd better not try to help me again," her friend said later. "I'm afraid if you come to my house, my husband will kill me."

A short while after this incident, officer Passarella was murdered. The neighborhood was shocked, but Maria had a different view of the tragedy.

"The Lord has said that the ungodly shall be destroyed, and you shall see it with your own eyes. The Lord be thanked for His help. It is not wise to do battle with the living God," she concluded.

DARKNESS HAD FALLEN, BUT MARIA WAS RELUCTANT to go inside from the porch where she sat. The evening was pleasant, and remembering the past blessings the Lord had bestowed on her, as well as the trials and dangers He had seen her through, brought comfort to her soul.

From the table, Maria picked up her thick journal next to her Bible. She flipped over the pages, but she didn't really need the reminders of the past that the journal contained. It seemed to her that some of the hardest burdens she'd been called to bear were the result of rebellion toward her from some of the church members.

As she held the journal in her lap, Maria laid her head back on the rocker and closed her eyes. According to her custom she talked to her Lord about her concern.

"I've put in a lot of years here, Lord. I've tried to do what you've led me to do each step of the way. Now some people don't want me to praise You out loud in the church services or to say 'Amen' when the preacher speaks. They try to explain that the times are different. New people don't understand, and they consider my praises a distraction in the service. But Lord, I believe You are the same, yesterday, today and forever. Your Word says that You inhabit the praises of Your people. If we do not praise You, the very rocks will cry out!

"I don't want to create problems in the services, so maybe this is the time I must praise You in my heart and worship You in my spirit. I am ready to do Your will as You show it to me."

Looking down the alley toward 20th Avenue, Maria's heart rejoiced at the sight of the Melrose Park Free Methodist Church, sitting solidly on the land that the Lord had pointed out to her 37 years ago. It was no longer an Italian mission, under the guidance of the General Missionary Board, but with the efforts of the Reverend Bush and young Tony Caliendo, had become a church in the Illinois Conference in 1942.

Maria remembered each pastor, and now as the evening darkened, she saw each of them again and recalled what she had recorded in her journal:

1. Angelo Previte (1925). An Italian young man from Pennsylvania who had just graduated from Greenville College. He preached very well in Italian, loved everybody. He married a beautiful young Italian lady after two years. She was civil in character, humble. After four years he returned to his home conference.
2. Brother Traina (1929). He was not ordained, an Italian who preached in Italian, but he held the doctrine of Moody Bible Institute, having been taught there. But we put him to preach, with the hope that he would accept our doctrine. He stayed five years. He was a man full of love, beautiful character, a precious man.
3. Dominic Mannoia (1934). He preached in Italian for four years. He would gather a large group of youth. He sacrificed himself for all of them. He had 120 in

Sunday school. He worked in the north side of Melrose Park, inviting children to Sunday school. He left to finish his work at Greenville College.

4. Brother Ed Boise (1938). A young man of excellent character, humble, and he loved us all. We have a great memory of him in that his first task was to build us a pulpit. It was made from a large table from which the Mannoias ate, and to this day it is still there. He redid the whole front of the church platform, the Sunday school roll, the illuminated sign in front of the church and a new room in the back where they lived. He had done a large work — more than any of his predecessors. He would go and visit the families with his wife. We always remember him. The Lord will repay him for his labor among us.
5. David Kline. With his wife and children. He would preach in English and work hard learning Italian. His wife was superintendent of the Sunday school. She had a good experience.
6. Brother Perkins. He and his wife were young and worked with the CYC, and with children at camp. They had a bent for finances, and to supplement their salary they worked as auto mechanics, renting a garage by the mission fixing cars and doing well financially, and the salary he received from the mission was enough to live on.

7. Brother Miller (1946). Then came Miller who stayed one year, his wife worked and received a good income. He had a good income from the mission, and having accumulated a good account, they left.
8. Reverend Bush (1947). He stayed for three years. A humble young man, patient, and visited the families and worked well for the Lord. His wife also was very good. When they left, we all were very sad to have lost them.
9. Brother Howard Wolcott (1950) for one year. He was a lively youth, very outgoing and gathered souls, working well. His wife was humble, sang special songs, and their time was too short. They were not able to stay on.
10. Brother Skene (1951). A wonderful young man, humble with the Lord and with all of us. He had a good voice and a tender heart. He respected all of us. His wife had a good experience working with children. This couple is with us now in 1952 [the year the journal was written]. They are acquiring new experience in the Lord's work to bring fruit for His glory.

WEARILY, MARIA ROSE FROM THE ROCKER, AND with her Bible and journal went into her familiar kitchen. She looked around the room, and it almost seemed that she could see them all — Papa, Rose, Dominic, Joe, Anne, Jimmy and Mary. Had it been worth it all? Had it been necessary to suffer all the abuse and persecution to reach the place she found herself today? For what would she exchange the salvation and ministry of her six children? Or the influence of the church on 20th Avenue? The precious hours of prayer and Bible study with her neighbors?

Nothing. There was nothing to exchange for those blessings from the Lord.

Maria sat down at the table and opened the journal to the last page. She would add one final paragraph for the glory of the Lord.

I pray for them all that the Lord will let them see the love of God, for who loves God loves his brother and sister. I thank the Lord that He has separated me with joy. I am content that I have fought and finished the course, I have kept the faith and now the Lord has prepared for me the crown for that day. Amen. Amen.

IN THE SPRING OF 1964, JOE MANNOIA RE-ceived a call from his nephew, Andy Scittine. Here is Joe's account:

"[Andy] said, 'Mama is looking bad.' So I got in my car and went to Melrose Park. Mama was looking real bad. I closed up the house, put her in my car and went to my home in Jackson, Michigan. I got the doctor to come to my home. Dr. Colletti was a very good friend. He wanted to know how long

Mama had this pneumonia. I told him I didn't know. Mama would never tell you she was sick. Every time I called her she said she was good, feeling fine. The doctor said we had to put her in the hospital. He called and the hospital said they would have a bed in the morning.

"Mama didn't want to go. I would put her shoes on, and she kicked them off.

"I said, 'Mama, you are making this very hard for me,' then I sat on the bed. She took my hand in hers and her last words to me were, 'Joe, *Io te amod.'* (Joe, I love you) and she went to heaven peacefully."

Maria went home to her Lord on April 28, 1964, 10 days after her 82nd birthday. It had been worth it all.